MY NAME IS AMERICA

The Journal of Patrick Seamus Flaherty

●●●●●●●●●●

United States Marine Corps

BY ELLEN EMERSON WHITE

SCHOLASTIC INC.
New York   Toronto   London   Auckland   Sydney
Mexico City   New Delhi   Hong Kong   Buenos Aires

This journal is based upon actual events, but all names and certain unit and operational details have been changed, in order to protect the privacy of the Marines who actually served so bravely at Khe Sanh. Although every attempt has been made to present the story as accurately as possible, based upon public records, any resemblance to actual people (other than public figures such as President Johnson) is very much a coincidence. When recounting the actions taken by certain soldiers, students of the Vietnam War may recognize the people they represent. As a result, no identifying details whatsoever are given, when these particular incidents are recounted, based upon after-action reports and other sources. All Americans owe a great debt of thanks to the veterans of the Vietnam War — and every other war.

Khe Sanh, Vietnam
1968

● ● ● ● ● ● ● ● ● ● ●

December 25, 1967
Golf Company, 3rd Battalion, 26th Marines
Khe Sanh Combat Base,
Republic of South Vietnam

Okay, so this was a *really* bad idea. Big mistake. Probably fatal.

Great. Or, as my little sister Molly would put it, *swell*.

A guy in my platoon was saying that you only have to be in Vietnam for about ten minutes to realize that you should never have gotten on the plane, gone through boot camp — or joined up in the first place.

Took me about ten *seconds*.

Give or take two or three.

But, think you'll hear me whining about it? Never happen, doggie. I'm a *Marine*. Semper fi, man. We *love* this stuff. War for breakfast, lunch, and dinner — and a little more thrown in for a midnight snack.

Even on Christmas.

Yeah, it's Christmas. I'm on a combat base, out in the middle of nowhere, surrounded by mountains, and jungle

— and, as far as I know, a whole lot of enemy soldiers. Or, anyway, so you hear. I've only been here for a few days, and I don't really know anyone yet. It's bad enough for it to be Christmas, but to be pretty much alone on top of it all? With no friends? Forget about it.

Lucky I'm so completely cool, or I might feel kind of sorry for myself.

I really don't want to keep a stupid journal, but — I promised. The Sunday before I shipped out (okay, okay, I *flew*), my father said he wanted to talk to me. Alone. But the Patriots were playing, and my uncles and a bunch of guys from Dad's firehouse were there, and I really wanted to watch the game. The last thing I felt like doing was going out to sit on the porch in the middle of winter. But I just said okay, and went after him.

So, we got outside, and it was really cold, and it looked like it was going to start snowing any minute. My father's a big, jolly guy, but once we were out there, he started shifting his weight and not really looking at me. He was in the Army in World War II, and fought from Italy, to France, and all the way to Germany. Except for funny stories about getting drunk with the boys and that sort of thing, he never talks about it, though. But I've always figured he must have seen some pretty bad stuff over there, because sometimes, he just gets this *look*. The same look he has after a really bad fire, when they don't get there in time to save everyone.

Finally, he cleared his throat and said, "Well, your

mother's really going to miss you. So you be sure and write her every chance you get."

I promised I would, because that's what he wanted to hear — and maybe I'll even do it. I wasn't so great about writing from boot camp, so I guess he figured I'll be that much worse in an actual war.

Then, we stood there some more, and it was just plain *cold* out there. Just as I started to talk about how I thought the Patriots are going to do in the second half, he took this little blue book out of his pocket. It was called *My Life in the Service*, and I could see that he had written his name in the front. The book had these sections called "My Buddies" and "Officers I Have Met" and "Places I Have Been." Stuff like that.

"I want you to take this with you, Patrick," he said. "Use it."

Sounded like homework to me — and if he thought it was such a hot idea, how come all the pages were blank? Turns out he filled up three of them while he was overseas, and this one was an extra.

"Do you still have them?" I asked.

He nodded.

"Can I read them?" I asked.

He thought about that, and then nodded again. "When you get back."

Since he had that *look* again, I didn't push it. But I kind of had to remind him that it's going to be hard to write anything honest, since Marines mostly only use one word — and it's really obscene. Come to think of it, that word is pretty popular around the firehouse, too.

"Pretend you think Molly's going to want to read it someday," he said.

Molly's my little sister, and she's a reading nut. Never goes anywhere without a book. She doesn't even brush her *teeth* without holding a book in her other hand. Smart as hell, that kid. Although she's fifteen now, and hates it when I call her "kid." So I do it constantly, just to bug her. Then, if I get bored, I think of stuff to bug my older sister, Brenda, too. Makes life pretty entertaining.

Anyway, I put the book under my arm, and we stood around some more. I was freezing, and I started to go inside.

"Patrick," my father said, and this time, he looked as serious as I've ever seen him. "When you're over there, make sure —" He stopped. "If things ever get —" He stopped again. "Don't think too much," he said finally. "Just do what you have to do."

I knew he meant it, and now I couldn't look at *him*. The idea of war seems a lot less scary when you aren't about to go off and fight one. And I'm the dumb, gung-ho idiot who blew off three football scholarships, went down to the recruiting station, and *volunteered*.

"Cold out here," Dad said, after a while.

So, we went back inside, and watched the rest of the game.

The Patriots got totally wiped out.

Later --

We just had a pretty decent chow. There isn't enough room for our battalion at the mess hall here yet, but they showed up with some containers of mashed potatoes, lukewarm turkey, gravy, and rolls. I tried not to think about the great dinner my mother would have made, and how we'd all be sitting around the Christmas tree, eating cookies and everything. Instead, I leaned back against some sandbags and ate next to my fighting hole. My squad was all sitting together, and I was close enough to listen, but not to participate, really. So far, I'm just the "new guy," and no one seems too interested in finding out anything more than that. They just call me "boot" and pretty much leave me alone. Hey, fine with me. The one thing I've definitely learned in the Marine Corps is that it's a lot easier to stay out of trouble if you keep your big mouth shut. Took me about ten thousand push-ups at Parris Island (in my platoon, we liked to call it "The Big P.I.") to figure that out, of course.

Every now and then, planes have been flying over the base here, playing Christmas carols over loudspeakers. The sound quality isn't so good, but I guess it's the thought that counts, right? The whole thing seems funny, but it's also a little creepy, in a way. Maybe we'll catch a break, though, and they'll drop a load of sugar-plums, or something. Uncle Sam's Misguided Children (yup, USMC), nestled all snug in their poncho liners.

Anyway, I'm not even sure what I'm supposed to write in this journal. I'd always get back my school papers with stuff like "Poorly organized!" and "What is your *theme*?" written across them in bright red. And usually, right next to that, was a big old "C."

So, okay. Just to make Mrs. O'Leary and all my other English teachers happy, I'll start off with a nice, little outline. Here goes:

1. I was born in Boston.
2. My parents named me Patrick.
3. I got older. Also in Boston.
4. I started playing football.
5. Now I'm in Vietnam.

Any questions? No, didn't think so. Wonder if I'd get an A for that? Probably not. Most likely, another C, and they'd put comments like "Flesh out!" and "More details!" in the margins. I might even get Mom's favorite: "Lazy work, Patrick! See me after class!"

Dad might be right — maybe I think too much. And about pretty dumb stuff, to boot. Not even Molly's going to be able to plow through *this*. But, hey, at least I'm keeping it clean!

So far.

I got in-country nine days ago. Which means I have 386 days to go before my tour is up. Not that I'm counting. Army mutts only have to serve a year, but Marines go for a full thirteen months. I figure that's just to remind the doggies that we're tougher than they are.

Which we are.

Goes without saying, right?

I guess I could write that we landed in Danang, but the plane pretty much *dove* straight down onto the runway. The guy next to me actually puked. Can't say I was too happy about that.

Getting off the plane felt like having an entire offensive line slam into you at once. It was so hot I swear I forgot my own name, and my uniform went from dry to soaked — and I mean, *dripping* — in maybe a minute. I was still pretty flipped out by the heat, when I suddenly noticed that the place just reeked, too. Man, talk about *funk*. Smelled like the whole country was one huge, open-air latrine. Plus, gasoline fumes, avionics fuel, motor oil, cordite, and fish that had been left outside to rot for the last six months. Any nasty smell you can think of was probably mixed up in there somewhere. On top of that, the sun was so bright that I instantly got a terrible headache, and had to use my hand to cover my eyes. Didn't help much. It was also really noisy and confusing, with planes and helicopters taking off all around us, artillery firing somewhere, and a bunch of sergeants and second lieutenants yelling orders at people.

And that was my first *minute* in the Republic of South Vietnam.

Then they had us stand in formation — in the sun, no water or anything — for what felt like about a month. A bunch of really grungy Marines were watching us and laughing and all. Wasn't too hard to figure out that they were on their way home. Their uniforms were all faded, they had on beat-up boots, and they had these unbelievable tans. Some of them seemed really hyped-up, or half-drunk, but most of them just looked tired. I knew they were probably about my age, but they looked older. *A lot* older. I felt like a jerk, standing there in my clean — not counting the sweat and vomit — stateside utilities. Might as well have been carrying a "Just Got Here and Don't Know a Freakin' Thing" sign. (See, Dad? I'm trying.)

There were a bunch of civilians around, too. A lot more than I would have expected. Maybe they were waiting to fly somewhere? I don't know. It was mostly women, avoiding our eyes and chattering with each other, plus a few children begging for candy and cigarettes, and some skinny little babies who were crying a lot. Have to admit, I envied the babies for being able to cry their heads off, without anyone looking at them funny. There were some South Vietnamese soldiers walking by, and I saw two of them holding hands, like they didn't even think it was a weird thing to do. Worst of all, there were a bunch of caskets lined up in neat rows near the tarmac, each one covered with an American flag. Looking at them gave me a stomachache, so I just closed my eyes.

We ended up on a bus, which took us to some reception center, so we could all process in. The windows were covered with these really thick wire screens. Turned out, that was so no one could throw grenades into the bus at us. Talk about giving you a nice, warm and friendly feeling about all of those civilians we were supposed to be here to defend.

The reception center was this big metal building, and the tin roof trapped all the heat inside, so that half the people standing near me looked like they were about to pass out. For the rest of the day, we waited in lines. Lots of lines. Filled out paperwork, answered questions, exchanged all our cash for this fake-looking military money we're supposed to use over here. They're called MPCs — military payment certificates, and it's like having a wallet full of Monopoly money. Don't figure I'll be shopping much, anyway, so who cares?

Lines, and more lines. Signing papers to designate your next-of-kin, so the Corps will know who to tell if you get killed, requisitioning ration cards, checking little boxes to say how much of your pay you want to have sent home and whether you're going to buy U.S. Savings Bonds — it just went on and on.

I saw one guy from my Infantry Training Regiment, and we gave each other a wave, but his name was called for the 1st Battalion, 9th Marines before we got a chance to talk to each other. Hope he does okay, wherever they send him. Some clerk told me I was going to the Rockpile up near the DMZ (which is what we call it, instead of saying "Demilitarized Zone" or the border between North and South Vietnam) to join my unit, but then another clerk came over and started arguing with him, saying that my company was at Khe Sanh now, not the Rockpile. They bickered about that for a while, and ended up telling me to come back in the morning. The whole time, I was standing there wondering how many IQ tests you have to flunk to get to be a clerk.

The mess hall had stopped serving right before I got there, and then I had a hard time finding a transit hut where I could rack out for the night. It made me pretty nervous that no one knew where I was — and more than that, no one *cared*. I also didn't like walking around without a rifle or anything. If we got attacked, what I was supposed to do — throw rocks at the enemy? I have a pretty good arm, but, *come on*. Down here, I think we're mostly fighting Viet Cong, but — yeah, we're lazy — we just say VC. Like instead of saying "North Vietnamese Army" to describe the enemy forces coming down from Hanoi and all, they're just the NVA. I was too tired to think about it much, though, and ended up in this crowded tent near the airstrip, lying on a stained canvas cot, surrounded by strangers.

A lot of the new guys were asking the Marines who were either on their way home, or coming here for their second tours, all kinds of questions. I barely had enough energy to halfway listen, but it was nice to find out that the explosions we kept hearing were *outgoing* rounds, not incoming. Some guy gave me a beer, and even though it was really warm, I drank it in about two gulps. Then I fell asleep, using my seabag for a pillow.

The next morning, after a lousy breakfast — powdered eggs, biscuits that weighed about two pounds each, and really bitter coffee — I stood in some more lines. Then, I ended up sitting on the metal floor of a C-130 plane with a bunch of other Marines, flying up to some base called Dong Ha. Once we got there, the lines and paperwork started all over again. At least I finally got issued some supplies — jungle boots, fatigues, flak jacket, the whole nine yards. The first helmet they gave me was all dented — I don't want to know how *that* happened — and the supply sergeant wasn't going to give me another one until I showed him that I couldn't even get it all the way onto my head. He did some complaining, but found me a replacement.

My "new" gun, an M-16, had some black tape on the stock, but when they took us to the range to test-fire our weapons, it worked just fine. Still, it didn't seem fair that they were giving us all of this secondhand stuff, instead of new equipment. I bet everything the *Army* gets is brand-new. I'm not so sure about the M-16, anyway — stateside, we did all our training with M-14s. This new rifle weighs a lot less, and feels like some kind of toy. I hear they jam a lot, too, if you're not really careful. Or really lucky.

We sat through some boring orientation lectures, and even had to watch a filmstrip about Our Wonderful Allies, and how we were going to help them preserve freedom and democracy. I figure that's true — why else would we be here? — but I didn't feel like seeing yet another film about it. We saw a bunch at Parris Island. Besides, I was still so tired that I just felt like sleeping.

It wasn't until the next afternoon that four other guys and me were told to go wait for this Sea Knight CH-46 supply chopper to fly up to Khe Sanh. One of the guys was on his way back from R&R, and I figured he knew what was going on. He seemed pretty salty, like they say, so I paid attention to the way he did things, in case I could pick up some stuff. Like he kept the chin-strap on his helmet unsnapped, and he covered the end of his rifle with a little piece of plastic. Since it was raining like crazy, maybe that was to keep it dry? Either way, seemed like a good idea to me. He also double-checked all of his grenades to make sure the pins were bent, so they wouldn't go off by accident, and put them inside pouches.

He saw me copying him, and grinned. "Not bad, newby!" he yelled over the sound of the choppers landing and taking off all over the place. "You might not get killed this week!"

Once we were in the air, it was too loud to talk, but the guy tapped his right boot with one hand, to show me the dog tag he had laced there. Then he pulled out the one around his neck, which was covered with black tape. Finally, he took out one of his M-16 magazines, held up ten fingers, and then seven fingers. In other words, only put seventeen bullets in, instead of twenty. I nodded, and the guy grinned again and made an "OK" sign at me.

The flight was noisy, and pretty rough. When we landed, the base was bigger than I expected. The salty guy said, "Semper fi, man," and then took off. That left me and the three other guys standing by the side of the airstrip, not sure what to do. A gunny came hustling over, and ordered us to help unload all of the ammo crates and C rations from the chopper, which took forever. Sergeants just aren't happy if they aren't telling someone what to do.

It was hard not to be scared, but everyone seemed pretty casual — flak jackets hanging open, rifles slung over their shoulders, that sort of thing. Their uniforms and boots were covered with reddish mud, and a lot of them hadn't shaved for a while. I asked a big blond kid where I could find Golf Company, 3rd Battalion, 26th Marines, and he wanted to know if I thought he looked like an information booth. I told him, no, he looked like a dumb hillbilly who was going to go home and marry his first cousin. So he called me a stupid potato head, and we kind of went at it. I managed to pop the guy a couple of times — and took a good one in the mouth, but the gunny broke it up pretty fast and swore at us a lot. Save it for the enemy, and all that.

By the time I got to Golf Company's part of the perimeter, on the northwest side of the base, it was almost dark. The skipper was all business, and told me to go check in with the third platoon and get squared away, because we were going on a five-day patrol first thing in the morning, and I'd be pulling perimeter guard on and off tonight.

Welcome to Vietnam, boot.

Later --

I don't have much time to write, because I have to go out on a listening post (LP) with the three other guys on my fire-team in a little while. We'll be maybe a few hundred meters outside the wire from 2200 to 0200. (That's ten o'clock until two in the morning.) The idea is to sneak out there, set up our position, and then wait to see if we hear anything or get attacked. If the North Vietnamese show up, our LP is pretty much out of luck, but at least we'll have time to warn the rest of the base. That's the theory, anyway.

We got in from our five-day sweep around the hills west of the base late this afternoon. The rumor is, we went all the way to Laos, but it's not like we got to a "You are now leaving Vietnam; Welcome to Laos" sign or anything. Basically, the whole patrol was what Marines call "a walk in the woods." And, mostly, a walk in the pouring rain. Whenever I heard a sound while we were out there, I was ready to fire off every round I had — or else, maybe just fall down and cry. But — nothing happened. No attacks, no shooting, no contact, no anything. It was pretty much just walking around this dark, prehistoric jungle all by ourselves. There are supposed to be tigers and elephants in this part of the country, but all I saw were monkeys and birds.

Except that sometimes, people found footprints. A few empty bunker complexes. And once, a pan of rice that was still warm. There were definitely enemy soldiers out there, but either they were hiding, or — I don't know. Kind of spooky. Nobody talked much, because we were out in the field and supposed to be observing noise discipline. I tried to watch all of the salts, and learn as much as I could. But, man, talk about *lonely*. I wrote about ten letters home, even though I know I won't get mail anytime soon, since my family probably doesn't even have my address yet. Which is really depressing.

I could tell that my squad was keeping an eye on me the whole time, trying to decide if I was a guy they could trust — and so, worth getting to know. Was I going to be the type who fell apart the first time we hit trouble, or would I suck it up and stay cool?

Wish I knew the answer to that one, myself.

My squad leader seems like an okay guy. He's a corporal, real thin and quiet and serious, named Rodriguez — except everyone calls him "Shadow." Everyone seems to listen up when he talks, so I figure he knows what he's doing.

Maybe I've seen too many movies, but have to admit, I was disappointed that we don't have a big guy named "Tiny," or a street-smart guy from Brooklyn. I mean, come on, what kind of squad is *that*? Actually, there weren't any Brooklyn guys in my platoon at Parris Island, either. When I went to my Infantry Training Regiment (ITR) program right after boot camp, though, we had one from the Bronx — and I figure that counts.

Lots of Southern guys in the squad. Lots of Southern guys in the *Marines*, for that matter. They call anyone from up north a Yankee. Which, as a Red Sox fan, really ticks me off. There's a tall, gawky all-elbows kind of guy from Kentucky who goes by the name Fox. I was sure there'd be some good story behind that, but turns out, it's just his last name. He's the squad's RTO — radio/telephone operator — which means that he carries the radio. Then there's a baby-faced black kid from Alabama — I figure he lied to the recruiters, and he's not eighteen yet — who answers to Mooch. Mainly because he's always hungry, and keeps trying to get people to give him any part of their C rations they aren't going to eat.

We have only one machine gunner right now — I heard the other one got hit by a sniper a few weeks ago. Apparently, he was still alive when he got to Delta Med, but no one knows what happened after that. Anyway, our M-60 man is this huge, loud, pug-ugly guy from Texas. In fact, his nickname is Smedley, after the old Marine bulldog mascot. I bet a hundred to one that he played football, but I haven't asked him yet.

So, go figure, me — usually the guy who talks his head off, and gets elected captain of the team, only now I'm feeling so out of it, I've barely even introduced myself to anyone. They all call me "Boot" or "Newby," although some of them just say, "Hey, you! Mick!" I don't even think I look all that Irish, but — okay. Fine. I heard it a lot at P.I., too.

The assistant gunner's a mean-eyed guy with a thick brown mustache and even thicker black-framed glasses.

He's from Baltimore, and his nickname's Rotgut. Apparently, even by Marine standards, he drinks a lot. From what they say, he'd chug down lighter fluid, if he thought it would give him a buzz. He spits a lot, too. Mr. Tough Guy.

Apollo is a stocky little black guy from North Carolina, who carries an M-79 grenade launcher. He thinks the space program is the coolest thing in the world, and wants more than anything to go to the moon — and maybe even Mars — someday. He seems pretty friendly, compared to most of the others, and even asked me my name once. He forgot it right away, but at least he asked.

Finally, there's the three guys on my fire-team. Hollywood is this really good-looking blond guy, who seems to have about five different girlfriends writing to him. Just looking at him, I thought he was from California, but I think he's actually from Colorado or Wyoming or someplace. Cowboy country. Professor is older than everyone else — I think he might be twenty — and he dropped out of college to join the Marines. Even our squad leader, Shadow, is only nineteen. Professor seems to be pretty smart, but maybe that's because he doesn't swear as much as the rest of us. Actually, Mooch doesn't really swear, either, and he's always reading from a bible.

I don't really like Bebop, the last guy in our squad, so doesn't it just figure that we keep getting put in the same fighting hole and on perimeter guard together? He's this lean black guy from Detroit, who thinks he's really smooth. *I* think he's weird, because ever since we got back to the combat base today, he's been playing on this clarinet mouthpiece he carries in his pocket. He can do lots of different notes, and scales — which I guess is cool — but every time he looks at me, I think he's going to —

Okay, that could have been ugly. Bebop just got in my face, wanting to know how come I keep looking at him, and if I hate being around brothers, like everyone else from Boston. I got mad, since that hadn't even crossed my mind — *and* I never told him I'm from Boston.

"Every time you open your mouth, we know you're from Boston," the Professor said, real quiet, behind us.

I don't even think I have an accent, so I don't get why people are always telling me that, ever since I joined up. If you ask me, *they're* the ones with accents.

"Come on, Boston, let's go," Bebop kept saying. "You think I can't take you?"

"Yeah, that's exactly what I think," I said. "So, back off, Motown."

Then Shadow came over. "What's going on?" he asked. "You got a problem, Boston?"

And I said that yeah, it was Christmas, I was in freakin' Vietnam, I suddenly seemed to have a really dumb nickname, instead of a cool one — and some kid from Detroit wouldn't shut up with his stupid kazoo already.

Just about the whole squad was standing around us now, and they all thought about that.

"Man, that is a whole lot of problems for just one guy," Apollo said, and even I laughed.

Hollywood's contribution was, "But hey, you got your health."

The malaria pills we have to take every day are making me sick. I'm covered with maybe a thousand mosquito bites, I've had a headache ever since I got in-country, and my boots don't fit. Good thing Marines don't complain, huh? So, all I said was that on top of everything else, no one — not even *one person* — in the whole squad had shared any cookies from their Christmas boxes with me.

Since it was true, most of them nodded, and then everyone looked at Bebop to see what he thought.

"It's not a kazoo, it's a *tenor sax* mouthpiece," he said, sounding really stiff. "And I'm sharing a hole with some dumb mick from Boston who never talks, and *I'm* stuck in frigging Vietnam, too."

Hard to disagree with any of that. Except maybe for the "dumb" part. I hope.

"Want some cookies?" Mooch asked, with a big grin on his little-kid face.

So, Bebop and I both had some cookies before we went out on LP with Hollywood and the Professor. It wasn't peace — but at least it wasn't war.

Merry Christmas.

• • • • • • • • • •

December 26, 1967, Hill 881S

I'm not sure anyone in the squad likes me, but at least they're talking to me now. Except for Rotgut, and I don't think he talks to anyone. Pretty scary, that guy — don't think I'd want him behind me in a dark alley. They're all calling me "Boston," and — well, it's better than "Mick."

I thought our platoon was going on patrol this morning, but then the skipper passed the word down that we were being choppered over to some hill outpost west of the base, instead. A lot of the guys who've been incountry for a while looked nervous, so I guess it's bad news. It's just going to be us, some real hush-hush radio relay team doing intelligence-gathering, an 81mm mortars platoon, plus some artillery guys with 106mm recoilless rifles and 105mm howitzers out there. So we're going from being on a combat base with a few thousand Marines and an airstrip and mess hall and aid station and all, to maybe a couple of hundred guys up alone on top of a hill about eight klicks away. That works out to about four miles, give or take.

Last spring, there were some really bad fights out here. There's our hill, 881S (for South), and Hill 881N, and Hill 861. You'd think they get more interesting names, but they use numbers, depending on how many meters above sea level each hill is. Since we're in the middle of the mountains, there are a bunch of hills, but those are the main three. I guess we lost a lot of good Marines during those fights. They won the hills, and took out a whole lot more enemy NVA, but — well, I hope it was *for* something, you know? I wouldn't have volunteered if I wasn't willing to die for my country, but if it happens, I want there to be a *reason*.

It's actually really pretty out here — all these rolling hills, and more colors of green than I even knew existed. But it's also way out in the boonies, and I'm not sure why we'd be fighting for a place that's pretty much deserted. The Professor says some Montanyard (Montagyard? Montangyard? I don't know. Never heard of them before.) tribes live out here, but that's about it. They're supposed to be on our side, and I think some of them are working as soldiers for the Special Forces guys at Lang Vei, down near Route 9.

It's Montagnard. I just asked. They're kind of like aborigines, in Australia, except they've been living in the mountains here for hundreds of years. Really primitive, traditional, able to take care of themselves. A couple of the guys who've been here for a while wear these metal bracelets the Montagnards make. It's this really sacred symbol of friendship and brotherhood, and even if they don't admit it, everyone wants one. (Can you tell the Professor just loves to tell you stuff? All you have to do is get him started, and he's off to the races.) Not that I mind, since I'm finally starting to feel like maybe I'm *part* of something here. It's put me in a whole lot better mood, I'll tell you that much.

Anyway, we got out here around 1400, and *boy*, were

the guys we replaced glad to be getting off the hill. I guess they've been here for a couple of months, or something. Their uniforms were plain *crusted* with red clay, and all ragged. And, man, oh, man, what a stench! Guess they didn't get a shower that whole time. Most of them had beards — if they were old enough to grow them — and they all seemed pretty wild and edgy. The whole top of the hill's not much bigger than a football field, and being out here alone must make you kind of stir-crazy.

Gee. Can't hardly wait to find out for myself.

Our platoon commander is a second lieutenant named Fanelli, and he started assigning us positions right away. He wants us dug in and set up before we lose the light. Plus, he wants us to check all the concertina wire around the perimeter, make sure the claymore mines are facing in the right direction — *away* from us — and that sort of thing.

It's not exactly raining today, but it's getting all misty and overcast. The choppers usually can't fly in weather like this, so we probably won't get any more supplies today than whatever's already here. Seems like we have a decent amount of ammo — hope we don't need it any time soon — but we'll have to make do with whatever C rations and water we brought along with us.

Better go dig for a while. More later.

• • • • • • • • • •

Around 2100

I've got blisters like you wouldn't believe. Not that I mind, or anything — nope, too tough to care — but I have to say, they're nasty. I spent just about the whole afternoon digging. The guys we replaced set up pretty decent bunkers, but they aren't deep enough. After a while, they must have gotten lazy, because there's also garbage all over the place. Empty C rat boxes and cans, old shell casings, smoke grenade cannisters, dud pop-up flares, stained bandages, empty bug juice bottles, lots of grenade pins, pieces of frayed comm wire, half-rotted web gear, dented M-14 and M-16 magazines — just a lot of junk. Guess they didn't care too much about policing up. Or else, they figured *we'd* come along and do it for them.

Looks like they guessed right.

We ate dinner sitting either on sandbags, or on top of our helmets. Hollywood showed me how to make a little stove, by using an empty B-2 can from my C rations. You cut off the lid with a P-38 (it's a little can opener — I keep mine stuck underneath my helmet band), then you make three holes down low in the can for ventilation. So, for once, I had a hot meal. Sort of hot, anyway. We have these little blue heat-tabs, which you can light and drop in the bottom of the stove. They take forever to heat anything up, though, so most of the guys use pieces of C-4 explosive. It looks sort of like white putty. You just tear off a little piece, light it up, and *whoosh*! Boy, does it burn fast and hot. You can boil up a can of water for coffee in no time.

I never drank coffee until I went to boot camp, but now I really like it. Maybe it doesn't always taste so great, but it sure helps keep you awake. I've seen guys just shake the little packets straight into their mouths and crunch it up dry — especially on guard duty.

C rations aren't that great, but they're okay. Besides, I'm usually so hungry that I'm not that picky. At home, when I'd get back after practice, I would sit right down at the table and drink a quart of milk, with a loaf of bread and peanut butter. After that, I'd be ready for dinner. My sisters thought I was a big pig — and I'd give them a nice round of burps, just to keep my reputation up. In the pig category, I'd say I'm pretty much undefeated.

Tonight, I had meatballs with beans in tomato sauce. I kind of scorched the bottom with the C-4, but I was able to scrape up most of it. People swap parts of their C rations for stuff they might like better, and it feels like the lunchroom at my elementary school, when no one wanted their apples. I finished up with crackers and cheddar cheese spread, and then some pretty foul fruitcake.

There are a bunch of huge rats up here — probably because the other unit left the place in such a mess. So, Lieutenant Fanelli told us to be sure and throw away everything in the garbage dump on the side of the hill. We're not supposed to leave out anything edible in our bunkers that might attract them.

I have to say, *I don't like rats*. Don't like them *at all*.

We get a little package of cigarettes inside the accessory pack of our C rations — along with salt, sugar, coffee, matches, cream substitute, gum, and some toilet paper. (Not nearly enough, if you're sick from your malaria pills, but, okay.) The guys who smoke'll trade just about *anything* to get those cigarettes.

Except for me, Bebop's the only other one in the squad who doesn't smoke. Says he won't put anything in his lungs that might screw up his horn playing. Turns out, he's a really serious jazz musician and wants to go pro when he gets out of the Marines. That's why he's always playing around with that mouthpiece — so he doesn't lose his embouchure. Yeah, it's actually spelled that way — I had him write it down for me. Then, I double-checked it with the Professor, who said, yeah, I guess so.

If I'm going to be writing all this stuff down, maybe I should ask my mother if she can send me a little dictionary. Might as well try to spell things right, if I can.

The platoon doc just came by, handing out vitamins and all. He's this pale, skinny guy, with glasses that are taped on both sides, but everyone says he's really brave when things get hot. Marines don't have their own medics, so Navy corpsmen get assigned to us. I think they'd probably rather be on their ships, but here he is. Bebop took out his mouthpiece and reed, and got Doc to pour some hydrogen peroxide on them. He says they get all mildewed, because of the weather. Not that he probably wouldn't stick it in his mouth, anyway, but might as well *try* to keep it clean, right?

Hollywood offered me a can of pound cake for my pack of Newports — and hey, I'm not stupid, I *took* it.

"So, what's your excuse?" he asked, lighting up. "Real Marines smoke."

"Football," I said. "I got a couple scholarships waiting at home, and no way I'm screwing up my wind."

Smedley was cleaning his M-60 — which he does about ten times a day — but he definitely perked up. "You play football?"

I just *knew* that guy was another football player. There's guys who were on their high school teams, and then there's guys who are *players*. Totally different animals. "Linebacker," I said. "And tight end, on the other side of the ball." I went to a small enough high school so that a lot of us got to play both offense and defense. No argument from me! Just meant more time on the field.

"You any good?" he asked, real suspicious. I'm just over six feet, and a hundred eighty pounds, but he's got about three inches, and maybe forty or fifty pounds on me.

I actually think I'm really good, but you can't come right out and *admit* that. It isn't cool. "On the sea, or on the land, I got the situation well in hand," I said.

Mooch laughed right away, and then some of the others got it, too.

"You are some kind of sucker, Boston," Bebop said.

Well, that didn't sound too good. "How come?" I asked, eating my pound cake. I should probably have saved it — but I was too hungry.

"'Cause you just gave yourself your own nickname, moron," he said.

Oh, shoot — he was right. I *am* a sucker. I have a feeling it's going to stick, too. Forever.

Forget Boston, forget Mick. Now everybody calls me. . . . Mighty Mouse.

Swell.

December 29, 1967

Haven't written for a couple of days, because we've been busy digging in and going on patrols and everything. The platoons are all going to take turns going on sweeps of the area, and today was ours. On days your platoon doesn't patrol, you're taking turns doing things like night ambushes, or LPs. If you're inside the wire at night, you take bunker guard duty. That's two hours on, two hours off, until morning. So, no matter how the schedule works out, you don't end up getting much sleep. The patrol schedule varies, but there's always at least one platoon up here on the hill to keep the area secured. The skipper seems to be really fair about how he divides things up, though, so can't complain about that.

That's not true — we all complain a lot, but nothing out of the ordinary. Our packs are too heavy, we're tired, there aren't any girls around — the usual stuff. If someone put me in charge, I don't think I'd worry unless my

Marines *stopped* complaining. Then I'd know something was up.

Girls. There's a depressing thought. Everyone else seems to have a girlfriend — or a wife. Mooch looks about ten years old, and he's *married*. It's not like I ever had trouble getting dates — I was co-captain of the football team, and hit clean-up on the baseball team, so I went out a lot. I just never fell hard for anyone.

Big lie. I did. I was just too stupid to ask her out. Her name's Audrey, and she went to my high school and goes to our church and everything. She's really smart, and didn't exactly hang out with the cheerleaders and girls like that. And she's pretty, but not tight-sweater *vavoom* pretty! So I wasted a bunch of time thinking it wouldn't look cool if I asked her out or anything. That the other guys would make fun of me for dating a brain.

Hey, for all I know, she would have said no, anyway. I was a big, dumb, loud football player — not her type. She went to the prom with this guy Keith, who was on the chess team. Math team. Debate team. Not exactly the kind of teams that would want me. Not that I'd want them — but, it'd go both ways, for sure. I think he went to Columbia. I know that he didn't get into Harvard, because he was really mad about it.

He was one of the people who really gave me grief when he heard I was joining the Marines. I've known him since third grade, so he must have figured I wouldn't mind if he told me I was an idiot and wasting my life for nothing. How wrong the war is, that soldiers are just tools of the government, and a whole bunch of stuff like that. I just said, hey, my father served, my grandfather served, my uncles served — it's what Americans are supposed to do. If they ask, you go and serve your country — it's our duty. He thinks the best way to serve your country is to let the government know when they're doing something wrong. I don't know. I would have hit him, but he's half my size, and besides, we were in Cub Scouts together.

And he's probably still dating Audrey. Lucky jerk.

Enough about all that. The patrol today wasn't too bad. I was scared the whole time, waiting to get attacked, but we didn't have any contact at all. There were some trails, which seemed to have been used recently, but there was no sign of actual *people*. I walked either behind, or in front of, Shadow all day, because he wanted to watch and see how I do things. Every so often, he'd check and make sure the selector switch on my rifle was set on safety, or that I wasn't walking too close to anyone, and that kind of thing. It's called keeping your intervals, when you spread out like that. You're supposed to stay far enough apart so that if a grenade or mortar round lands, a whole bunch of us won't get killed all at once.

The platoon gunny was watching me, too. He's this tough old bird named Sampson who fought in Korea *and* World War II. Chews tobacco, carries a flask, barks at us a lot — everything you expect in a gunny sergeant. You can't not admire the guy.

The only thing that happened all day was that a guy in the second squad banged into a beehive somehow. His face was so swollen from stings that you couldn't really see his eyes, and they'd gotten him through his uniform, too. Doc was afraid he might go into shock, so the LT called in a medevac for him. The rest of us got all cut up from walking through the elephant grass, but that's an everyday thing. Before I got here, you never would have been able to convince me that grass can actually be *sharp*. But I've got the cuts to prove it. It also grows about ten feet high, so you just end up buried in the stuff — can't even see where you're going.

When we got back to the hill, there was mail waiting for us. Except that I didn't get any. *Again.* Don't they have my address yet? What's taking so long? I've already sent out about fifteen letters. We don't have to pay postage — gee, thanks, Uncle Sam! We just write "Free" in the corner of the envelope, where the stamp would go, and drop our letters in the company mailbag. Then, whenever a chopper comes in for resupply, or a medevac, or something, we throw the mailbag on. So, why don't they write to me already? Don't they miss me?

Hollywood felt sorry for me, so he let me read his mail with him. Four different girls! And four different kinds of perfume! Wow. Pink stationery, light yellow stationery, stationery with puppies on it, and stationery covered with roses.

"Are you dating *all* of them?" I asked.

"Sort of," he said, shuffling through the stack. "But I didn't get one from Lori today, and I think she's my favorite." He handed me the yellow envelope. "Here, read Vicky's. She always puts in great pictures."

I opened the letter, and — he wasn't kidding. Vicky was blonde, and tan, and wearing just about the smallest bikini I ever saw. "How do you keep them all straight?" I asked, checking the photograph from every possible angle. Purely scientific interest, you understand.

Hollywood grinned. "I just use Honey, and Baby, and Darling, when I write," he said. "That way, I can't screw up, and use the wrong name by mistake."

Not the guy you'd want dating your sister, but definitely impressive, no two ways around it. "You're a god, man," I said. "An absolute *god*."

Funny thing — he didn't deny it.

December 31, 1967

It's New Year's Eve. I'm in Vietnam. Nobody in my family has written to me.

Think that just about says it all for today.

• • • • • • • • • •

January 1, 1968

We started off the New Year . . . with a patrol. No contact, no sign of any NVA — not even any footprints. Same old, same old. But even I noticed that it seemed a little *too* quiet. Fewer monkeys chattering, not so many birds. That can't be a good sign. I happened to meet Shadow's eyes at one point, and he just looked grim and tapped his nose. In other words, they're here; he can *smell* them. We just never actually *see* them. So far.

The word is, that the NVA is building up thousands of troops somewhere out here, and that sooner or later, they're going to attack us. They want the main combat base, but they'll probably take out the hills, first. Which means us and 861, plus the radio platoon up on 950. 881N is still Indian Country. We haven't found them yet, but — I don't know. We must be doing all of this patrolling for a reason. If no one was out there, wouldn't they just ship us someplace else, instead of wasting time here? We're close enough to the border, so that maybe they're spending most of their time over in Laos. But then, why did we see all those bunkers and footprints on that five-day sweep? You always hear that the NVA and VC are really into tunnels, so for all I know, they're *underneath* us. All this waiting is scary. You wish they'd just make a move, already. Get on with it.

For the first time, I saw a village. It was Bru tribesmen, from the Montagnards, and not at all what I expected. For one thing, some of the women weren't wearing shirts!

And some of the others had their blouses unbuttoned. That is *my* kind of town. For their culture, it's completely normal, so I tried to pretend I didn't even notice.

Not sure how successful I was at that, but I gave it a go.

I've seen Vietnamese villages on the news on television, so I pictured little thatch huts and rice paddies and nervous VC sympathizers treating us like an invading army. But these Montagnards were smiling! They actually seemed happy to see us. Most of the men wear loincloths, and carry cross-bows, and it all seemed like something out of *National Geographic*. I wish I'd had a camera, because it was really interesting.

Their houses were built up on stilts; I'm not sure why. To protect them from flooding, during the monsoons? A couple of the children were grabbing at me, and it was making me sort of edgy — until I figured out that they wanted to touch my skin, because it's white and looks so different, and maybe hold my hand for a minute. When I started thinking of them as enthusiastic little kids, like my niece and nephew, I relaxed. This wasn't the kind of village where some six-year-old was going to throw a grenade when my back was turned.

I could hear Bebop playing nursery rhymes on his mouthpiece, and a bunch of little kids were watching him with amazement.

"Hey, they like your harmonica!" I said.

He grinned. "Shut up, Mighty Mouse," he said, and went back to playing.

One thing for sure, the climb back up to 881S after these patrols is *tough*. It's really steep, and if there's been any rain at all, it gets so muddy that sometimes you slide back ten steps for every two steps you take. All I wanted to do when we got back to our bunker was fall down and sleep. I didn't, because we had to unload some ammo crates and a bunch of other stuff, but I was *really* dragging. And don't let anyone tell you that flak jackets and helmets aren't *hot*. After spending all day hacking our way through triple-canopy jungle, bamboo, thorns, deep streams, and all that, that final hump straight uphill is a real killer.

At least last night was a little bit fun. Battalion sent out some cans of eggnog, and there was enough so that we all got to have some. Can't say it was *delicious*, but who cares? It was eggnog. We would have liked it better, if they'd sent some whiskey to put *in* the eggnog, but that didn't keep anyone from drinking it up.

Then, at midnight, the skipper gave the okay for a mad-minute. In other words, we were allowed to fire our weapons like crazy. I blew off two magazines in less than a minute. We also shot up a bunch of flares, and the artillery guys shot off some illumination rounds. It was really loud, because the guys over on 861, and down on the main base, and even over at Lang Vei to our south, were doing the exact same thing. All the red tracers — we always load them into our magazines, every fifth round or so — looked neat slicing through the night. Like tiny little shooting stars, or something.

If the NVA *is* out there, they must have been really confused to hear us all go crazy like that in the middle of the night. And it was really fun for us. When you think about it, sometimes the whole Marine Corps just seems like Boys with Toys, you know? Big shiny weapons that make really loud noises and we can even make things explode and cool stuff like that. Last night, we got to play with our toys — and nobody got hurt. Sounds like a win-win situation to me.

Hope it's always that way.

January 2, 1968

I had the worst possible C ration meal tonight — ham with lima beans. Apollo let me borrow some Tabasco sauce, but it didn't help. I also had some canned white bread, which tastes like glue, even if you heat it up. And applesauce for dessert. Terrible meal, all the way around.

Not that I didn't finish every bite. Every bite just tasted lousy.

I heated up a can of cocoa after that, and thickened it up a little by adding a packet of cream substitute. While I was drinking it, I was looking at Bebop, trying to figure out what he had written on his helmet. Most guys put their hometowns on the front, and their girlfriends' names, and stuff like that. But, his had other stuff.

He put down his spoon, halfway through a can of fruit cocktail. "What?"

"Is Trane John Coltrane?" I asked.

Bebop pretended to be shocked, and allowed as how yes, it was.

"So, who's Jug?" I asked. "And Prez?"

Bebop closed his eyes. "You don't know the first thing about jazz, do you?"

Hey, I thought I was doing pretty well by guessing Coltrane.

"Don't *even* tell me you don't know who Bird is," he said.

I don't know who Bird is.

Bebop groaned and closed his eyes again. In fact, he fell back against some sandbags and covered his face with his arms. "Gene Ammons, Lester Young, Charlie Parker," he said through his arms. "Coleman Hawkins, Ben Webster, Johnny Hodges." He lifted one arm enough to look over at me. "Let me know when I hit one you know."

I gave him an okay sign. He ran through a *really* long list of names — and I gave him a thumbs-up when he said "Benny Goodman." I knew Louis Armstrong, too.

"Figures," he said, and flopped down again.

So I started reeling off football players — throwing in some pretty obscure ones, I have to admit — and he finally raised his thumb when I said, "Johnny Unitas."

Which gave me a chance to point out that he didn't seem to know a single damn thing about sports.

"Jackie Robinson," he said. "That's enough for me."

So, just to make sure that I had gotten him good and mad, I rattled off about twenty players from the old Negro Leagues — and Satchel Paige was the only one he knew.

Hollywood was listening to all of this, laughing and shaking his head. "This is just getting ugly."

I *did* have one dumb question left. And I was curious, so I figured I might as well ask. After all, he was *already* pissed off. "What's 'bebop' mean?"

Bebop groaned, and stamped off into our bunker in disgust.

I *really* have to get a dictionary one of these days.

January 4, 1968

We had guard duty on the base today, instead of going on patrol, so I spent some down time personalizing my helmet, writing on the cloth camouflage cover with a black pen. I drew a kind of lame picture of Mighty Mouse flying along one side, with his cape whipping out behind him. Then I put "Go, Red Sox!" on the other side.

"What's BFD?" Apollo asked, when he saw what I had written on the front.

"Boston Fire Department," I said. "My father's on the job."

"Okay," Apollo said, and grinned. "If you say so." He

had "FTC" written on the front of his, which he said meant "Fun, Travel, and Comrades."

When a resupply chopper showed up later and dropped off a mailbag, I got twenty-three letters. Twenty-three! Wow! My mother, my father, Molly, Brenda, my Aunt Kelley, Father McDougal from St. Anthony's, Mrs. Rollins from down the street, Harry — my best buddy from the football team; he's going to the police academy now — wow! I feel rich.

"So, someone does like you," Bebop said. "I'd about given up."

He'd about given up?

With so many letters, I wasn't even sure where to start. I wanted to take it slow, enjoy every single word. I guess I didn't *really* think no one's been writing to me — I know better — but, well. . . . The letters were full of news — and full of questions. Where I am, if I'm okay, what I'm doing, if I'm okay, if there's anything I need, what it's like, and if I'm okay.

"Poor little Mighty Mouse," Mooch said. He had come over behind me, and was reading over my shoulder. "Tell them you need Tabasco, and Kool-Aid, and all the food they can fit into a box, so you can share with me."

Kool-Aid would be great, actually. Iced tea mix, maybe, too. The water tastes so awful, especially after we add the purification tablets, that people use Kool-Aid to try to make it easier to get down. Of course, when you're thirsty enough, that's not a problem.

"If there's one from a girl, you have to let me read it first," Hollywood said, lounging against some sandbags a few feet away.

I like Hollywood a lot — but let him anywhere near my sisters? Even with Brenda already married? Not a chance. So, I handed him one from my grandmother.

"You're a funny guy, Mighty Mouse," he said.

Bebop was playing low, slow notes on his mouthpiece — long tones, he calls them — and looking grouchy. I think he's the only one in the squad who didn't get mail today. So I gave him one of Brenda's and told him to read all about my niece and nephew. He actually looked pretty happy about that, stuck the cap on his mouthpiece and put it away in his shirt pocket.

Hollywood wandered over. "You get any *pictures* of girls, at least?"

I passed him a photograph of my dog (okay, okay, my sister's dog, but I love her, too) Maggie. She's a black setter mix, really sweet, and I think about as pretty as a dog can be. But, when it comes to dogs, I'm the guy who actually cried when I saw *The Incredible Journey*. That old Bodger really got to me.

Might not share that with the guys. But the other night, when we were talking about movies, just for fun I told them I cried like a baby at the end of *Mary Poppins*. Even Rotgut laughed at that one.

"Is she a good dancer, at least?" Hollywood asked, handing Maggie's picture back.

Oh, yeah. My dog can really cut a rug.

Twenty-three letters. Wow!

January 5, 1968

A guy in first platoon got bitten by a rat last night. He woke up, and the thing was sitting right on his chest! Said it was about as big as a cat, which I believe, because these jungle rats are *monsters*. I pretty much sleep with one eye open — and keep my Kabar knife handy, just in case. You can hear them squeaking and squealing all night long. They fight like maniacs, too, so maybe they *are* rabid. Scary. He was medevaced out, and will be gone for ten days for treatment. Apparently, you get the injections in your *stomach*. Sounds terrible.

We also had four new replacements come in. None in my squad, but one got assigned to my platoon. Having replacements show up is good — it means I'm that much further away from being "the new guy." Now, *they're* the new guys. Until the next wide-eyed boot in clean fatigues shows up.

Shadow and Rotgut have been here longer than anyone else I know, and they got here last summer. Most of the rest of the guys came in-country during the last two or three months. That makes me feel better, since it means they're not *quite* as salty as I first thought. Most of us signed up right out of high school — or as soon as we turned eighteen. And yeah, most of us fell for the "Let the Marines make a man out of you" line. The Professor is almost twenty, so he's an old guy around here. He dropped out of Northwestern University, because he didn't think it was fair that people who couldn't afford college were getting drafted. That makes him cool in my book — even if he *was* majoring in philosophy.

I was asking Bebop how come he's not in the Marine Corps Band. Seems like he ought to be. He says the last thing they want is a hard bopper (whatever that means), and besides, he doesn't "look right." Meaning that he's not white, I guess. And, the truth is, like me, he kind of wants to fight.

Well, no, it's not that we *want* to fight, we just — okay, I admit it. Part of me really *wants* to fight. Find out what kind of man I am. Or even *if* I'm a man. I mean, that's why you sign up for the Marines, right? Not to sit behind a desk somewhere, filing papers or handing out supplies or something. Yeah, you also sign up to serve your country, but if that's all you wanted, you could be a squid, or a doggie — or even ride around with the Coast Guard.

But it must be really awful if it turns out you're a coward. Better to know, I guess, but you'd just spend the rest of your life all ashamed. The *last* thing I want to do is let down the guys. I'm probably supposed to want to fight for God and country — but I really just want to make sure I'm there to back up other Marines.

Sometimes I'm really scared. Especially at night,

alone, on guard. Or when we go on night ambushes. I'm not sure what's worse — when it's all foggy and you can't see anything, or when it's clear and *everything* looks like a bunch of enemy soldiers sneaking up on you. Shadow says you should just keep your eyes moving smoothly, and not focus too long in one place. That way, you'll notice if something in front of you changes or moves. I hope.

I learned how he got his name the hard way. A couple of nights ago, I was on perimeter guard, and suddenly, he was standing right next to me in the fighting hole. I didn't even hear him coming over — the guy just appeared out of nowhere. So, that's why they call him Shadow.

We're heading out on another LP now; I'd better go get ready.

January 7, 1968

Used my weapon for the first time. I mean, for real — not just a mad-minute, or test-firing. We were on patrol down on the west side of the hill, and I saw movement off to the side in this bamboo thicket. I took maybe half a second to think about it, switching my rifle from safety to automatic. Then, whatever it was came leaping right out towards Apollo and I blew off a full magazine without waiting to see what it was. The whole platoon dropped in place, and there was a whole lot of shooting and yelling for a few minutes. Gunny Swanson had to scream "hold your blank-ing fire!" about ten times before anyone listened. LT was running back and forth, trying to figure out what was going on, and who had started firing first.

Rotgut was behind me, and he grabbed me by the collar, growling something about "stupid boots who get everyone else killed." And Apollo was really mad, since I had fired right next to him like that and almost scared him to death. Shadow and Gunny Swanson came back to yell at me, too, and I was trying to tell them that I was sorry, but I'd seen something move.

Right around the time Lieutenant Fanelli showed up to do some yelling of his own, Fox suddenly said, "Oh, man, look at *that*."

Apollo leaned forward, and there, maybe a foot away from his leg, was this huge cobra. An actual *cobra*. Neck puffed out, mouth open, fangs extended, like it had been just about to strike. I must have hit it a few times, because it was all bloody, but it was still moving. Rotgut whacked its head off with his machete, and then we all just stood there, staring at the biggest, ugliest dead snake I ever saw. The thing must have been twelve feet long, maybe more.

"Looks like Mighty Mouse was on the job!" Hollywood said, all cheerful.

Apollo had this sick expression on his face — and I didn't feel so hot myself. That would have been a really bad way to go. Not that any way is good — but, still.

"Enough eye-balling, ladies," Gunny Swanson said. "Let's saddle up!"

So, we moved out. The rest of the patrol was routine, but I was still creeped out, even when we got back to the hill.

I bet Apollo was, too.

January 9, 1968

I'm getting mail pretty much every time resupply delivers a bag now, and that makes being here seem a whole lot easier. I also got a package from my mother with brownies, LifeSavers, a Red Sox cap (I'm wearing it right now), some blank stationery, a couple of pens, a toothbrush, and other great stuff. My father even cut a bunch of articles out of the *Globe* about the Patriots' games I missed, and the play-offs. Smedley grabbed the ones about the Dallas Cowboys, and hasn't brought them back yet. The rest of the squad went through my brownies so fast that I only got three. Tasted really good, though — not stale at all.

A funny-looking little new guy got put in our squad. Seems like a nice kid, but really uncoordinated, and has trouble with easy stuff like using his P-38 to open his C rations and filling sandbags. He actually keeps *missing* the bag with his shovel. About nine times out of ten. But it's hard not to like a guy who says stuff like "Oops!" when he screws up. Mooch named him Pugsley, after the roly-poly kid in the Addams Family. Suits him.

Got a great letter from Molly today. She promised, before I left, that she'd write to me what was really going on at home, and I could write her the real truth about anything that happens here. But, if it's something bad I don't want my parents to know, we agreed that I'd mail it to her friend Theresa's house, instead. Any letter I send to my house, I know the whole family'll want to read.

She's still doing some moping about this guy Jason she's liked forever. I think he's a punk, and not good enough for her. If I told her that, she'd probably just like him more. She says Mom's going to Mass every single morning, and if Dad's not at the firehouse, he goes, too. I guess they're really worried about me. She also wrote that she wanted to start volunteering at the animal shelter, but they won't let her, because they're afraid she'll try to bring too many pets home. She's always finding stray animals — which is why we have three cats, and our dog Maggie. Most of our relatives have at least one stray from her, too. I wonder if —

Later --

Had to go help some of the guys in one of the other squads with their bunker. Half the roof just caved in on them. Turned out, the timbers they'd been using for overhead cover had been eaten almost all of the way through by termites. The skipper keeps asking the main base to send us up some stuff to use for overhead cover, but they won't do it. And the engineers won't come and cut down trees for us, because their chainsaws keep breaking. During the Hill Fights last spring, I guess most of the trees got hit by shrapnel, and when the saws hit the little pieces of metal, they get wrecked. A lot of the trees were destroyed back then, and you see jagged, broken trunks all the time. We run into a lot of old bomb craters, too, when we're patrolling. The jungle is growing right back over most of them, but some of the others have turned into really foul-smelling little ponds.

What a mess that bunker was. One guy named Baretto was still in there when it happened, and we had to work fast to dig him out. He got lucky, though — the way everything fell, he was in a pretty big air pocket. So, he's even more filthy than the rest of us, but he's fine.

We haven't had much rain, which is good, because then *all* our bunkers would probably collapse. The sky is almost always grey, though, and we have lots of fog. Actually, it's not always fog — sometimes, we're actually inside *clouds*, because we're so high up. But when it's clear, we have this really amazing view for miles around. Green hills, mountains, waterfalls — it's like a nature film.

Except for the fact that there are cobras down there. And maybe the NVA.

We look down right over the main base from here. The airstrip is the biggest thing there, but even from four miles out, we can see the whole place really well. Compared to our tiny little hilltop, it looks like this really great city you wish you could visit sometime. The guys down there get showers, hot meals, and movies almost every night. They're still probably finding stuff to gripe about, but up here, we call the main base "Summer Camp."

If you look north and west, you see Hill 881N, and more mountains behind it, spreading all the way to the DMZ and Laos. Down to the south is the Special Forces Camp at Lang Vei, and further up Route 9 towards the main base is Khe Sanh Village. A bunch of Vietnamese civilians live there. The other day, Shadow pointed out this one place down near the village which is actually a French coffee plantation. Here, in the middle of a war zone.

Wish they'd roast some beans and send them on up to us.

Our hill has a higher peak, and then a lower one, with some lower ground they call a saddle in-between them. Sometimes we use the saddle for one of our landing zones, but the main one is up at the top of the hill. Our platoon is spread out along the north side of the hill, so we look straight out at 881N. Hill 861 is just off to our right, maybe a thousand yards away. It's a little too far for us to be able to wave at the guys over there, but sometimes, when we get bored, we try to signal each other with flashlights or mirrors. Kills some time.

Our whole company is spread out into a full defensive circle around the hill. The Command Post, the mortar and artillery guys, the howitzers, and the ammo bunkers are all inside the circle, for protection. When we go on patrol, we leave through the main gate on the far west side of the hill. Except that it isn't very far, because the whole hill is — like I said before — about the size of a football field. But it sure seems a lot bigger at night, when it's so dark you can't even see the guys in the next *bunker*, forget the next platoon.

Man, am I hungry. I'm really thirsty, too — they never send us enough water up here. Bebop heard that a guy in 1st Platoon got a box full of salami and pepperoni from his parents today. We're going to go see if we can scrounge some from him — especially since we have C rat cigarettes to trade.

Boy, would I give a lot if I could walk down the street to Harvard Avenue and get a nice, hot pizza right about now. . . .

January 10, 1968

Hollywood's dead. I can't believe it. My God, it was awful.

Bebop and I were out by the perimeter, stringing some fresh layers of razor tape, and trying not to shred our hands in the process. We were arguing about something stupid — can't even remember what it was right now — and goofing around a little, too.

The skipper wants us to have trench lines connecting all of our positions, just in case, so Hollywood was working on that. We already have some trench lines finished, but we're supposed to make them deep enough so that we can use them to walk around safely even if we get attacked. I think the Professor was digging inside our bunker, but I'm not sure.

Out of nowhere, there was this big explosion behind us. Dirt, and rock, and maybe shrapnel, were landing all over the place, and Bebop and I hit the deck. We both got tangled up in the concertina wire, and my ears were ringing because the explosion was so close to us. So there we were on the ground, trying to untangle ourselves without getting cut up worse — and still stay low, in case there was another explosion or we were under attack. There was a lot of yelling around the perimeter, as people tried to figure out what happened.

Then, we heard it. Real soft, real calm, real sad.

"Oh, God," someone was saying over and over. "Oh, no. Oh, God."

It was Hollywood's voice, so Bebop and I forgot about the razor tape and went leaping back to our bunker. Took less time than it did to write that sentence. Hollywood was on his back in the dirt, and at first, we thought he was okay — until we saw that his legs were gone almost all the way up to his hips, and one of his arms was all ripped up, too.

Bebop started yelling for a corpsman, and I could hear a bunch of people running towards us. Hollywood was just lying there, blinking a lot. There was so much blood I didn't know what to do, but I bent down next to him, anyway. Held the hand that didn't seem injured, while I used my free hand to try and rip off one of my cargo pockets and maybe use the cloth to slow the bleeding down.

He knew who I was, but other than that, he was really out of it. "Am I hurt?" he asked.

"No, no, you're going to be fine, buddy," I told him. "Everything's cool."

He smiled at me, a little, but his voice was so quiet that it was like he was disappearing right in front of me. "Am I okay?"

Inside my head, I was screaming, but I smiled back at him. "You got it," I said. "Just take it easy. Doc's coming over. You're going to be —"

He looked down at himself, at what was left of him, and the weird part was that he didn't even seem surprised. Or scared.

"Wow," he said, really, really quiet. "What a mess." Then he just — closed his eyes.

I was still holding his hand, and talking to him, and I guess it took about three guys to pull me away, so that Doc could get through. I can't really remember. Doc started slapping pressure bandages onto the wounds and began to get an IV going. Then, almost as quickly, he stopped, and just rocked back on his heels. Stared at him, without saying anything.

I knew it wasn't right for Hollywood's head to be resting in the dirt like that, so I shoved my way back over there.

I sat down on the ground, and held his head as gently as I could. I think I was talking to him again, in case there was still some part left that could hear, but I'm not sure. There was a lot of activity going on around us, but I just concentrated on keeping Hollywood company. No way was I going to leave the guy alone. Not my friend. No chance.

"Patrick," someone said.

It had been so long since I'd heard my first name that it seemed unfamiliar.

"Patrick," Bebop said again. "We have to move him, okay?"

We had to move him. Okay. So I helped move him, helped put him in a body bag, and helped lift him into the medevac which flew up from Charlie Med a while later. No one said a word as we watched the chopper lift off.

The skipper asked me if I needed some time, and I said, no, sir. So he put me and Bebop on a detail filling sandbags to build up the protective wall around one of the howitzers. It was probably a good idea, since neither of us felt like going back near our bunker yet. Doc told us we both needed stitches for some of the cuts we'd gotten from the concertina wire, but we kept filling sandbags. Didn't talk. Didn't look at each other. Just kept digging.

I never saw anyone die before. I hope like hell I never do again.

Hollywood was a great guy.

January 11, 1968

When resupply came in this morning, Doc — and the LT — ordered me and Bebop to get on and fly down to

Charlie Med, which is what we call the battalion medical aid station on the main base. There didn't seem to be much point in arguing, so we climbed aboard, along with a guy from the artillery battery who'd been running a really high fever and shaking all night.

No one's exactly sure what happened to Hollywood, but they think he must have hit an old mortar round left over from the Hill Fights. The blast hole had been so big that he couldn't just have dropped a grenade or something by accident. The round had probably been a dud that landed in the mud and had gotten buried just deep enough for us not to know it was there. During monsoons and everything, it would have sunk in even further. Then, when Hollywood hit it with his shovel, the freakin' thing detonated.

Can't get too much more random than that. Makes the whole thing seem even worse. If that's possible.

We got to Charlie Med during base sick call. The guy with the fever was in pretty bad shape, so they took him first. Bebop and I didn't much feel like talking to anyone — we haven't been talking at all since yesterday — so, we sat off by ourselves. The other Marines were wearing helmets and flak jackets the same way we were, but they looked different. For one thing, they were a lot cleaner. I looked at Bebop, and realized we weren't a black guy and a white guy — we were two *red* guys.

After a while, a guy sat next to us who had hurt his ankle *playing Frisbee*. It actually looked like it might be broken, and probably hurt a lot, but *Frisbee*?

"Y'all come down from the hills?" he asked, with this real heavy Southern accent.

Made us sound like wild animals. I just shrugged, and Bebop said "unh-hunh," in this flat, mean voice.

The guy was a Marine, though, so he didn't scare off quite that easy. "What's it like out there?" he wanted to know.

Bebop and I looked at each other. New guy. Definitely a new guy. And we were both too mad at the world right now to be nice to him.

"We love it," Bebop said.

"Can't get enough," I said.

The guy finally figured out that maybe he ought to leave us alone, and he limped off to sit somewhere else.

I felt a little guilty — but not much.

In the E/R, they shot us up with a bunch of penicillin and we both ended up with about twenty-five stitches, each. The worst cut I had was this gash on my calf, although I had a pretty deep one on my left palm, too. Bebop had a bad slice on his arm, and they stitched up one on his cheekbone, too. The smaller cuts we had, they just cleaned up and taped or bandaged, depending on the size. They said we could probably take a couple of days back in the rear at Dong Ha, if we wanted, but we just shook our heads. They all seemed to think we were crazy to say no, but who cares? They didn't watch *their* buddy go home in a bag yesterday.

Then we couldn't find a ride back to 881S. It was getting late in the day, and nobody seemed too interested in two grunts who wanted to get back to their lonely little unit in the hills. We waited around the airstrip for a while, then finally gave up and went back to the aid station.

Things were pretty quiet at Charlie Med, since sick call was over, and one of the corpsmen managed to find us a couple of clean T-shirts to put on under our filthy jungle jackets, and some fatigue pants which weren't exactly clean, but were in better shape than the ones we had on. We were also each given a bottle of antibiotics to take for the next week, so that the cuts will be less likely to get infected. Or, anyway, not as *badly* infected.

There was a chaplain just coming out of the sick bay, and when the corpsman told him we were stuck here overnight, he found us a couple of empty racks in a tent near the airstrip. I think most of the guys who lived there worked in helicopter maintenance. The chaplain also made sure we had a couple of canteens and some C rations. Before he left, he asked us if there was anything we wanted to talk about. We said no, but we were polite about it, since he was a chaplain and all. He'd also been really nice to help us out.

It was a lot more noisy on the main base than we were used to on the hill, because there were so many different kinds of outgoing artillery firing missions constantly. Just about everyone seemed to have a radio or a tape player, too. Some of the guys on 881S have radios, but the reception kind of comes in and out, and the batteries don't last too long. Down here on the base, a lot of places even have *electricity*. Whole other world. Summer camp.

Bebop asked around to see if anyone *anywhere* had a jazz tape he could listen to, but all people seemed to have was country and rock and roll. So, since we were really tired, we went back to the maintenance tent to get some sleep.

I was just dozing off, when I heard some guys talking about the Super Bowl. Green Bay is going to be playing the Oakland Raiders. Oakland has a solid team, but Bart Starr and the Packers should roll right over them. In my opinion, anyway.

When I remembered that I still had a bunch of football articles from my father in my shirt pocket, I got an idea. I asked if anyone was interested in some articles from the States about the end of the season and the playoffs. They all were, and I was able to swap the whole stack for an extra T-shirt to bring back to the Professor, a carton of cigarettes for the rest of the squad, and — best of all — two cans of Schlitz beer. So what if they were warm?

"That was pretty good, Patrick," Bebop said, sipping his beer. "First class scrounging."

I nodded, also sipping. I was going to take it slow, and make the beer last for an hour, if I could.

Might be a long time before either of us gets another one.

• • • • • • • • • •

January 12, 1968

In the morning, the whole base was fogged in, so there were no flights going in or out. The fog didn't burn off until early afternoon. We finally ended up on a chopper with some cases of C rations, an overstuffed red mailbag, a resupply of M-60 ammo and 81mm mortar rounds, and a guy from second platoon who was on his way back from R&R. I only knew him by sight, but that didn't stop him from showing us some — well, pretty personal — pictures of the new lady friends he'd made in Taipei.

Bebop and I didn't mind at all.

When we got back to the hill, there was some new guy sitting outside our bunker, eating a can of C rat turkey loaf.

"Who's the newby?" Bebop asked, when we gave the Professor his T-shirt.

The Professor had already torn his old T-shirt off and was putting on the new one. "Name's Perez. Doesn't speak much English, but he seems okay."

The Mean Green Machine sure hadn't waited too long to send a replacement. Out with the old, in with the new. Just makes you feel warm all over.

Gunny Sampson was handing out our platoon's mail, and when he pulled out a pink envelope, we all knew whose letter it was. He frowned and started to tuck the letter into one of his cargo pockets. Shadow asked if we could have them, instead, since his family had probably already heard, but they might not know how many girls he was courting through the mail. This way, we — well, probably the Professor — could write nice letters back to each of them. Otherwise, they'd probably find out when their letters came back stamped "KIA." Killed in action. Or, in this case, killed by a completely stupid *fluke*.

So Gunny Sampson gave us all of the letters from girls, while Lieutenant Fanelli took the three from his family. He and the skipper were both going to have some tough condolence letters to write, too.

Hollywood's real name was Steve, and looking at the return address on one of the letters, I found out that he was from a little town in Oregon.

And, like I said before, he was a great guy.

January 16, 1968

Things are heating up. Every day, we're seeing more of our planes doing bombing missions out in the mountains. Sometimes they fly so low they're actually below the top of our hill. Hope they're actually *aiming* at something, and not just firing at random. Fly-Boys with Really Big Toys. We've also had a bunch of recon guys chopper up from the main base every couple of days, and then run intelligence-gathering patrols from here. A couple of reporters have even shown up, to take pictures and everything.

We went on patrol again today. If nothing else, all this humping with 75–80 pounds on your back is a serious workout. Sometimes my back and shoulders ache so much afterwards that I feel about sixty years old. The salts say we do a lot more climbing out here, but at least it's not as hot as it is near the coast. I *still* think it's pretty hot, especially on the valley floors, underneath all that jungle growth. One of the other platoons found a bunch of footprints and fighting holes yesterday, but we struck out again. Just another walk in the woods.

Fox was able to rig up an antenna to a transistor radio, so we could pick up some of the Super Bowl. There was a special broadcast on AFVN Radio for "the American fighting man." Green Bay won big over the Raiders. Listening to football made me *really* homesick.

I wish I'd gotten a scholarship to Notre Dame. If I had, I would have gone there, instead of joining up. But I guess being one of the best players in the Boston public high schools doesn't quite cut it there. I could have applied, and maybe tried to make the team as a walk-on, but — I don't know. Figured my odds weren't too good. I probably should have gone ahead to Boston College. Practically in my backyard, lots of people I know go there, a great football team. And with me being a local guy, they knew about me and were definitely interested. Syracuse would have been okay. Penn State, too. Even if I had to start off being second-string. And at places like Holy Cross and Trinity and Assumption, I would have been a star player. But, for some reason, I had my fool heart set on Notre Dame.

What an idiot.

Smedley wanted to go to Texas or Texas A&M, but

when the coaches worked him out, they said he was too slow to play at that level. So, he decided to be a Marine, instead.

We're both idiots.

January 18, 1968

Today, we went out on another patrol near 881N, and one of the recon teams tagged along with us. They peeled off when we got about two-thirds of the way out there, to do whatever it is recon guys do. In the meantime, we finished our sweep of the area and headed back to the hill.

Didn't see anything. Didn't hear anything. Didn't run into anyone. Which was all just fine with me.

But then, the recon team radioed the CP to say that they were in trouble. I guess they hit an ambush, because most of them were wounded, and two guys got killed. None of us were surprised when Lieutenant Fanelli volunteered our platoon to go back out and get them. We were going to have to move fast, so orders were to leave everything but our weapons and ammunition behind. No packs, no food, no flak jackets. LT told us to bring a couple of canteens each, but any other extra weight was just going to slow us down. Most of the platoon wore boonie hats, instead of helmets, too. I don't have a boonie hat, so I stuck on my Red Sox cap. Gunny Sampson gave me a look, but he didn't say anything about it.

Then, we headed out, fast. In fact, we flat-out *ran*. That steady, even pace I remember from boot camp. We've been patrolling so often during the last few weeks, that we're all in really good shape. We've also spent enough time around 881N to know where we're going out there. The jungle slowed us down more than once, but we made pretty good time. Whenever we could, we ran through streams or down trails — it was much faster that way.

Fox was monitoring the company and platoon radio frequencies, and I was close enough to be able to hear a lot of the conversation. The recon guys sounded like they were really having a tough time.

We expected to run into the middle of a battle, but the NVA had already withdrawn by the time we found the patrol. Lieutenant Fanelli checked his map to find a decent-sized landing zone, so he could call in a medevac. Most of them were too badly hurt to walk, and the bigger guys in the platoon teamed up to carry them.

Rotgut and I went over to a huge guy who was all shot-up and lifted him in a sort of fireman's carry.

"You done this before?" Rotgut asked suspiciously.

Even a *crisis*, the guy never let down. I told him my father was a captain in the Boston Fire Department. He actually seemed to like that answer, and we carried the guy without any more conversation. The recon guy was half-unconscious, so he wasn't talking, either.

Once we got to the LZ, we let the corpsmen handle

the casualties. The rest of us formed a defensive perimeter to try and secure the area. My adrenaline was really pumping, because I expected half the NVA to walk up on us any second. Shadow came darting by to remind everyone in the squad to drink some water, so we wouldn't pass out. I sucked down a whole canteen in about thirty seconds.

I felt as though it took hours for the medevacs to show up, but it was probably more like twenty minutes. We sent out the most seriously injured recon members first, and then another chopper came in for the two KIAs. The recon guys who were "walking wounded" were going to come back to the hill with us to report in to the CO.

It was another super-fast hump through the jungle to get back to 881S before dark. I noticed that both Pugsley and Perez were keeping up with the rest of us, so from now on, they probably aren't going to be considered new guys.

The last twenty-four hundred feet — the climb up the hill — were the worst I ever remember. We were all breathing hard and perspiring so much that it looked as though we'd been out in the pouring rain. Man, after a day like today, I'll never complain about two-a-day summer football practices again.

Once we got through the main gate, a few guys dropped right in their tracks and some of the others bent over and started throwing up. The rest of us kept putting one foot after the other until we made it to our bunkers. *Then*, we fell down. Or threw up.

"That was . . . a day," Bebop said, panting.

"That was a day and a *half*," I said.

The skipper came by later and thanked each of us in the platoon individually, which I thought was cool. Said we were damn fine Marines, and he was proud to be our commander.

Didn't make us any less tired — but it was still cool.

January 19, 1968

Word is, the recon guys left a radio out there yesterday — and a bunch of code sheets. Since recon usually acts like they're much better Marines than us poor old grunts, there was a lot of bitching about having to go out and clean up after them. At least one of the other platoons got the assignment this time. It doesn't bother me that they dropped the radio — hey, people were shooting at them — but how hard is it to jam a few code sheets into your pocket?

While they were out there looking, 1st Platoon ran into an ambush. We were all ready to saddle up and go after them, but I think 2nd Platoon would have gotten the call, instead. 1st Platoon was able to make it back on their own, though. Our arty (artillery) and mortars guys were firing like crazy the whole time — artillery rounds from our 105mm howitzer guns, and 60mm and 81mm mortar rounds — sending supporting fire out there for them.

When it was all over, there were a few WIAs, and one

guy — a machine gunner — got killed. I guess he was laying down cover fire, so the rest of the platoon could pull out safely. I didn't really know him, but I still feel terrible about it. He was definitely a hero to do that.

This war is getting scary.

January 20, 1968

It's 0430, and we're pulling out soon. The skipper is sending the whole company out, including the 60mm mortar guys, to find — and eliminate — the NVA who have been around 881N for the last couple of days. Since we can't leave the hill undefended, two platoons from Hotel Company were choppered up here. They'll cover our positions, while we're out in the field.

We're going to move out while it's still dark, try to get a jump on them. Everybody's packing as much ammo as they can carry. Most of us even have LAWs — light anti-tank assault weapons. The terrain's too rough for tanks, but we can use the LAWs to take out bunkers. If we need them. Grenades, bandoliers filled with magazines for our M-16s (except for the guys who are still carrying M-14s), extra belts of M-60 ammo for the machine guns, bayonets, Kabar knives, even a shotgun or two. But, it doesn't feel like Boys with Toys this time — it feels like Men with Weapons. Nervous men, but men. If they want to take us on, we'll be ready. I hope.

Last night, I wrote letters to everyone in my family, just in case.

I have a bad feeling about this one.

January 22, 1968

For the first time, I think I really understand that I'm in a war. A *bad* war.

I don't know where to start, so I guess I'll just try to go in order:

We left the hill right before dawn. That was two days ago, although it feels more like a *year*. It was very foggy, and the ground was slippery. I don't think anyone ate breakfast before we pulled out. There wasn't really any conversation, either. Bebop and I made some coffee, and I got down most of a cinnamon nut roll. He ate a couple of crackers with some peanut butter. Right before we left, I saw him slip his mouthpiece out of his pocket and hide it inside the pack he was leaving behind in our bunker. I knew he was embarrassed that I had noticed, so I looked away.

"What do you want, man? That's an *Otto Link*," he said. "You know how expensive they are for a guy from Tan Town?" "Tan Town" is what he calls the ghetto.

Well — pretty expensive, I guess.

We were on our way out of the bunker, but I stopped and grabbed a couple of photographs — one of my dog, and one of my niece and nephew in their Halloween costumes.

(A really small fairy princess, and an even smaller Batman.) I took my helmet off, and tucked them in underneath the liner — I'm not sure why. Just wanted them with me, I guess.

It was really foggy. You couldn't see guys standing ten feet away from you. We were going to go out in two columns. Our platoon would be leading one of them, with a recon team and some 60mm mortar guys behind us. The other column was going to be the 1st Platoon, with the company command group behind them, and 2nd Platoon bringing up the rear.

Pugsley was in the column right in front of me, and he kept shifting his weight back and forth and swallowing so hard that it was really getting on my nerves. I told him to cool out, that this was just another walk in the woods. That didn't seem to help any, so I gave him a couple of pieces of C ration gum. Figured it would calm him down. Instead, the smacking and chewing started driving me crazy.

For some reason, the fog made every noise seem that much louder. The way we were all breathing seemed almost like screaming to me, and when the dew dripped off the elephant grass and vines, I swear it sounded like a waterfall. I think I was just concentrating so hard that my hearing was better than usual. I also kept shivering — which I hope nobody noticed. Probably not, since most of them were too busy being scared themselves.

By the time we got to the bottom of the hill and were moving through the valley, the fog was — if possible — twice as thick. We had to slow down even more, just to keep from getting separated. At this rate, it was going to take us a week to reach our objective. Up ahead of us, the 105mm howitzers and the 81mm mortars from 881S were firing what they call "artillery prep to soften up the area." Basically, that means you try to blow up — or scare away — as many of the enemy as possible, before the infantry troops got there.

Finally, around 0900, the fog began to burn off a little. The sun was coming out, and the temperature jumped from chilly — to steaming hot. But since we could see where we were going now, we picked up the pace. When we got to the bottom of 881N, Lieutenant Fanelli told us to take a quick rest break.

I sat down on a rock and stared at the ground between my boots. For some reason, I really wanted a cigarette, even though I don't smoke. Not that any of us were supposed to smoke when we were out in the field, because the enemy can smell it. I drank some water from one of my canteens, then checked my rifle to make sure it was clean and ready to go. Checked it twice, actually. Back on the hill, we had all taped a few of our magazines together in pairs. That way, if you fired one, you could just flip it around and have another full magazine ready to go in seconds. So, I checked them, too.

Way too soon, the order to "Saddle up!" was whispered back along the line. I remember I felt a little dizzy, so I took a couple of deep breaths before moving out. We made our way along the ridge, heading up the smaller hills leading to 881N. Everything seemed quiet, and I began thinking that this really *might* be just another one of our walks through the jungle. We climbed up out of the last of the fog, and the sun was brighter than I expected it to be. I slowed down, blinking to help my eyes adjust.

The first cracking sound confused me. I thought a tree limb must have snapped off nearby or something. But then, it turned into one long stream of gunfire, and I heard the whooshing and explosions of RPGs being fired. It took me another few seconds to remember that I should hit the dirt, *pronto*.

We were out in an open area — mostly just elephant grass, no good places to take cover. The NVA had us pinned down, and a bunch of people were already yelling "Doc!" and "Corpsman, up!" I was just lying there, pressed into the ground. More than anything, I wanted to run away, or crawl into a hole, or — around about that time, I remembered I had a rifle. In fact, not only did I have a rifle, but I could actually start *firing* that rifle.

Which I did. I didn't know exactly where to aim, so I just fired in the general direction up ahead of us. The NVA must have been within throwing distance, because chi-com grenades were falling all over our position. One landed so close to me that I knew I was dead. It hit the ground with a thud, and I automatically covered my head with my arms and waited for it to go off. I counted to five. To ten. To twenty. No explosion. I lifted my head just enough to see the grenade lying a couple of feet away.

"Throw it back!" Rotgut bellowed.

Okay. Why not? I grabbed it by the wooden handle and whipped it back in the direction it had come from as hard as I could. But I had to get up partway to do it, and as I started to flop back down, I felt this really hard thump in my side.

I was hit!

I fell over and felt all of this liquid spreading across my left hip. *Damn.* I was lying there, really mad, swearing my head off. They actually *shot* me. Took me a minute to get the nerve to look down and see how bad it was.

Make that, how bad it wasn't. A bullet had hit one of the canteens hanging on my web gear, and the water had spilled all across my front. I was really happy for a second, and then I was scared again, because bullets were still flying all around me.

Rotgut was yelling for me to move up, but I could hear other voices screaming "Pull back! Pull back!"

Nothing made sense. Everything was so noisy and confusing that I couldn't think. I rolled into a prone firing position and wondered where to aim. About half of the platoon was in front of me — I think — and I didn't want to hit anyone.

Rotgut was on his feet, advancing in a crouch, and I followed him. He'd been in-country so much longer, he'd have to know where to aim, or — he suddenly went down with a yelping growl. Then he ran off a string of what my grandfather would have called "champion cussing," and staggered to his feet. He made it another three steps before he got hit again.

I called for a corpsman as I low-crawled my way up there. Not that anyone was going to hear me, over all the shooting and everything. He had been shot in the right leg, and the bottom of his face was covered with blood. It looked as though a bullet had gone right through his cheek. He was spitting out blood — and what looked like a couple of teeth — and trying to get up. I was shouting at him to stay down, so he wouldn't get *me* shot, too. His response was to swing at me and for an injured guy, he packed a lot of power. Got me right in the nose.

There was a field dressing stuck underneath his helmet band and I yanked it out. I was going to tie up the wound on his face, but he looked so terrified that I realized he might choke on blood, if I did. So I tied it around the bullet wound in his leg, instead. It didn't stop the bleeding, but it maybe slowed down a little.

Thud! Another grenade landed somewhere very close, and I threw myself on top of Rotgut to cover him. A few pieces of shrapnel clattered off my helmet and slammed into the back of my flak jacket. I felt something burning on my arm and shook it off without taking time to see what it was.

A bunch of guys were running past me down the hill. I guess the Marines would call it withdrawing — but it was more like a completely panicked retreat. I mean, they were dropping gear right and left, without even seeming to notice.

A hand fastened around the collar of my flak jacket, and my first instinct was to fire at the person.

"Flaherty! Get Rotgut out of here!!" Lieutenant Fanelli ordered, crouching down next to me. "Toss a frag and a smoke out there, then bring him back!"

Now Fanelli turned to yell at everyone else. "Covering fire, people! Mooch! Perez! Grab that ammo!"

My reactions felt really slow — but I don't know, my sense of time was all screwed up. I wasn't sure if we'd been pinned down for five minutes — or five *hours*. I'm still not sure, actually. I wrenched a smoke grenade from Rotgut's web gear, and helped myself to one of his baseball grenades, too. He tried to swear at me through his mangled mouth, but just gurgled something I couldn't understand.

I threw the frag, then followed it by popping the smoke grenade — and the billowing yellow smoke made everything seem even more unreal. I was afraid to stand up, but what choice did I have? I closed my eyes and hoisted Rotgut up over my shoulders, while he groaned and tried to punch me again. His helmet fell off, but I didn't stop to get it because I was already trying to carry both of our rifles with my free hand.

And — we pulled back. Broke contact. Disengaged. Ran away.

Final score: NVA 1, Marines 0. *Damn it.*

I'm really tired. I'll write some more later.

Around 2000 --

We've been working on our trench lines all day. In the back of my mind, I can't help wondering if I'm going to dig into a live round the way Hollywood did. But you can't think that way, or you might as well just shoot yourself in the foot and try to get them to send you home.

Which a guy in 1st Platoon did last night.

I didn't know there were NVA graves up here, back from the Hill Fights, until a guy in the second squad dug into one by accident the other day. I was upwind from him, and the stink was still enough to make me gag. The more digging we do, the more often it happens. There's nothing you can do, other than hold your breath, bury them again — and go dig someplace else.

A month ago — maybe even a week ago — I wouldn't even have been able to imagine something so horrible. Now it's all just part of this stinking lousy war, in this stinking lousy country.

I can't even remember where I was in the story before. I'm so tired.

Rotgut. Right. I carried him back to this LZ, where the corpsmen had a casualty collection point. Apparently, the 1st Platoon had also run into trouble over on the other ridge, because I could hear a bunch of firing and artillery coming from that direction. Someone told me that the NVA had shot down the first medevac that flew in, but they moved the LZ further back and more were coming in.

The point guy from our third squad had been killed in the first few seconds of the fire-fight, and we'd had nine other guys wounded. Of course, I already knew about Rotgut, but it was really bad to see Apollo on the ground, covered with frag wounds. I think he caught a bunch of shrapnel from an RPG. Doc said it looked worse than it was, and he should be okay. I was going to go over and talk to him, but a chopper came in, and he and Rotgut were both gone before I even had a chance to say good-bye.

"You all right, Mighty Mouse?" Doc kept asking. "You hit anywhere?"

He was trying to shove a dressing onto my face, and I realized that Rotgut must have given me a bloody nose when he slugged me. I told him I was fine, and poured some water onto the dressing so I could wipe away most of the blood.

I found Bebop and the Professor slouching inside an old bomb crater with Pugsley and Perez. Nobody looked like a new guy today. They were all smoking — even Bebop, and I sat down next to them.

"Give me one, too," I said.

They gave me one. We smoked. It was really hot. We weren't under any cover, so the sun was just beating down on us.

"You hurt?" Bebop asked.

"Nope," I said. "You?"

He shook his head.

"You hear Grady bought it?" the Professor asked.

The point guy from the third squad. I nodded.

"He never got to see his baby," the Professor said. "She was born two months ago."

That just made me feel even more tired.

Artillery missions were being fired right over our heads, landing further up 881N. There were jets flying missions, too, dropping bombs that made the ground shake underneath us. We sat there, waiting for orders to head back to 881S and regroup. Instead, Shadow came over and told us that the word had come down, and Battalion wanted us to take the hill. I think we all wanted to refuse, right then and there, but nobody did.

Lieutenant Fanelli had us form up in a tight defensive perimeter in one of the bomb craters, while he showed us where he wanted us to go, and how he wanted us to do it. We were going to try flanking the NVA position, and see if we could surprise them that way. Most of us were pretty low on ammo, and Gunny Sampson redistributed what we had left, so we would each have the same amount. The medevacs were supposed to resupply us with ammunition, but it had all been on that first chopper, which got shot down.

Most of the third squad had been wiped out, so LT put them together with the recon team to make a new squad. Our squad and the second squad were still in pretty good shape, and we were going to take the lead this time. Smedley was the only machine gunner left in the platoon, so he was going to be carrying a lot of the load. His jaw was set really tight, and I knew he was grinding his teeth, so that no one would be able to see that he was afraid.

Like we weren't *all* afraid? I walked over to stand next to him for a minute.

"The Cowboys suck," I said.

He laughed. "Who went to the play-offs this year, hunh?"

The Cowboys.

At the last minute, Lieutenant Fanelli told us to "fix bayonets." That meant that he wanted us to resort to hand-to-hand combat, if necessary. A lot of us just stared at him, but he repeated the order and we attached our bayonets to the ends of our rifles.

"Anything happens, write to my mom, okay?" Bebop muttered into my ear.

I nodded. "You, too."

He nodded back.

I wanted to take out my pictures of Maggie and the kids, but there wasn't time. If I didn't make it out of this, my niece and nephew were so little that they probably wouldn't even remember me. I'd just be poor Uncle Patrick, who died in Vietnam.

LT called in one more fire mission to the big 155mm howitzers down on the main base. We were going to assault, while the artillery — I hoped — kept the NVA's heads down. Even though they seemed to bounce right up and start shooting again, no matter how many bombs and mortar rounds landed on them. The first and second squads would do a standard fire-and-maneuver, while the new third squad went up around our right flank.

Goes without saying that the plan didn't work. I don't think we got fifty feet before the NVA opened up on us with everything they had. Their machine guns were really doing a number on us. But Fanelli just wasn't going to let us stop. He took the lead — and hey, we followed him. Every time he yelled, "Let's go!" we went, firing our weapons and throwing grenades — and yeah, using our bayonets — until the NVA were forced to fall back from their positions.

And then, right at the top of the hill — they got him. He dropped in his tracks so fast that I knew he was dead. Gunny Sampson immediately took over — and they got him, too. Shadow had already gone down, and then I saw Smedley collapse, still firing his M-60 until he hit the ground. There were a bunch of snipers somewhere, just picking us off, one by one.

We were at the top of the hill, but another couple of NVA machine guns had opened up on us from the east, and everyone scrambled around to find cover. Most of us ended up crouching in the same fighting holes the NVA had just abandoned.

"They're right over there!" Pugsley shouted, one position away from me. "Lay some fire into that tree-line!"

Pugsley? Wasn't he supposed to be crying and flipping out right about now?

"Mighty Mouse, go get the pig!" he yelled. "You're on the 60 now!"

Was this really *Pugsley?* "Who died and put you in charge?" I yelled back.

"Look around — they're *all* dead," he said. "Now, go get the pig, you stupid jock!"

Doc had dragged Smedley into a mortar round crater, but the M-60 was just lying out there in the open. I was sick of hearing Pugsley's voice, so I vaulted out of my fighting hole and ran out into the line of fire to get the machine gun. Bullets were hitting all around me, and I dove back into the hole head-first. I hadn't fired an M-60 since I did my staging training at Camp Pendelton right before I shipped out. I knew how they worked — but not very well.

There was half a belt of ammo left in the gun, and I was wearing a spare one over my shoulders. If I was careful, I might be able to make them last — a minute or two. I fired short bursts — just two or three rounds at a time — and yelled for anyone who had ammo to throw it over.

Didn't know they were all going to take that literally.

The rest of the afternoon was a blur. The executive officer of the company came running over from the command group on the other ridge and took charge. Right away, he started re-directing our fire and told us to dig in. There weren't enough of us left standing to make another assault, but the 2nd Platoon showed up to reinforce us. The skipper was in the group, too, and he assumed command, calling in more air strikes and artillery barrages. The jets even dropped napalm, which landed so close to us that the heat blistered the tops of my arms when I ducked down. But the NVA never seemed to stop firing at us. The napalm started a bunch of fires in the elephant grass, and the smoke was really thick. It made me think of my father, running into burning buildings, day or night, never thinking about his own safety. I *was* thinking about my own safety, but I was thinking about everyone else's, too. That was enough to keep me in my hole, switching back and forth between my rifle and the M-60 to conserve my ammo, doing my best to stop the NVA every time they counter-attacked us.

The third squad with the recon guys was missing, and the LT from 2nd Platoon was all set to lead a rescue party. It was really brave — but he got wounded on his first trip down the ridge, and died from a bullet to the head. So his platoon sergeant plunged down the side of the ridge by himself to go find the rest of the missing guys. He came back carrying one, and said that the others were all injured — or dead. Turns out we'd driven the retreating NVA right through their flanking position. A few people went back with him to get the rest of them, including — this time, I wasn't quite as surprised — good old Pugsley. *That* guy is a *Marine*.

Man, I was *surrounded* by *Marines*.

With 2nd Platoon backing us up, we could have taken the rest of those NVA. I *know* we could have. But just as we were getting ready to assault, the word came down from Regiment Command for us to pull back and return to 881S immediately.

I was so pumped up that I thought I had heard wrong. Didn't they know that we were about to *win*? How could they call it off? We'd lost about half of our guys — and we were just supposed to *walk away*? Most of us were ready to go ahead and assault no matter *what* the brass said — but more air strikes were coming in, and the skipper got us focused on securing a new LZ and evacuating our casualties. We did it — but we weren't happy. And then some.

What was left of the company limped through the main gate on 881S right before it got dark. The battalion CO, and some other officers, were standing there waiting for us, but they knew better than to say anything. You'll never hear anything quite so loud as a bunch of absolutely silent — and completely furious — Marines.

I've had it. I'll write the rest tomorrow.

January 23, 1968

God, I'm tired. Bebop and I went out alone on an LP last night. We lost so many guys on 881N, that we've gone from 4-man LPs down to 2-man. So, from now on, we'll get to be twice as scared out there as usual, I guess. We thought we heard movement, more than once, but it was never anything definite enough to call in. We stayed on full alert all night long, watching and waiting, and expecting the whole NVA to open up on us at any moment.

No word on how many of the guys we evacuated the other day survived. From our squad alone, we lost Shadow, Apollo, Rotgut, Smedley, Perez, and Fox. Seven Marines died out there on 881N, and we medevaced about forty others. So, that just leaves me, Bebop, Mooch, Pugsley, and the Professor. Our new platoon commander — Gunny Kowalski from 1st Platoon — moved a guy named Twerp (guess why) from the 2nd Platoon into our squad. He got paired up with the Professor so that we'll have two guys to man each of our three positions. Twerp's pretty small, but I know he's a tough kid, because I saw him in action out on 881N. No worries there.

And even though I'm not really trained for it, I'm the new squad machine gunner. But you'd better believe I'm also going to hang onto my M-16. Can't have too much firepower.

Anyway, I never finished the story about that night (I guess it was the 20th?). When we got back from the battle, they gave us a couple of hours to eat some C rations and maybe grab some sleep. Then, the whole hill went on full alert. Obviously, the CP knew something we didn't. But that's nothing new. We just assumed they were expecting some kind of big attack.

Since we'd already had such an eventful day.

Bebop and I stood in our fighting hole, taking turns

sipping from a canteen cup of cold coffee. The hill went on 100% alert pretty often. It seemed darker than usual — maybe because I was so tired. Tired *and* wired. It wasn't raining, but there was lots of fog around.

I don't think either of us were ready to talk about the battle yet, so Bebop and I talked — really softly — about home. He's sure his girlfriend, Nina, is cheating on him, because when he first got in-country, she was writing to him almost every day. Now he's getting letters from her less and less often. The way I see it, the Corps doesn't even manage to resupply us with enough *water* out here. How likely is it that they're getting our mail to us on time, either? I also reminded him that I don't even *have* a girlfriend, so at least he has someone to miss. He didn't like that logic much, and when I thought it over, I wasn't crazy about it, either.

We talked about our families, too — more than usual. Bebop's sending most of his money home to his mother, so that she can pay bills, and the extra combat pay bonus we get *really* helps out. That made me feel like a jerk, because I'm so lucky. Yeah, I send almost all of my paycheck home to my parents, but they just put it in the bank for me. Bebop's father had a good job in one of the car factories up in Detroit, but he got hurt and can't work anymore. So, his mother is having a lot of trouble making ends meet — especially since Bebop has two little brothers, and a little sister, too.

He thinks Molly sounds maybe too smart (he's read a

couple of her letters), but definitely cool. I'd say he's right, in both cases. Brenda is cool, too, but in a totally different way. She married my brother-in-law right after she graduated from high school, and was pregnant by Labor Day. It's weird to think that she's only a little bit older than me, but already has a three-year-old — that's Jane, and a ten-month-old baby — Gregory. That's what she wanted, though. My parents weren't happy about it, because even though neither of them went to college, they wanted all three of us to go. Well, maybe that's *why* they want us to go. Looks like they're out of luck with two out of three of us, so far.

My father was pretty upset about Brenda getting married so quickly, because Hank is five years older than she is, and is one of the firemen in Dad's engine company. Brenda met him at a barbecue at the firehouse when she was only sixteen, and they fell for each other right away. Molly and I kind of had fun helping her keep it a secret until she was old enough to marry him. My father would *never* have given her permission to date someone that much older. My mother is pretty easy-going, but she wouldn't have liked it, either. I think Hank's a good guy, but my father always looks worried and says he takes too many chances on the job.

"You going to be a fireman?" Bebop asked.

Was I? "Probably, yeah," I said. "As soon as no one lets me play football anymore. Can you make a living playing the sax?"

"Yeah," Bebop said. "Lots of cats do. Just not a real *good* living."

"Well — I'm going to buy all your albums," I said.

Bebop laughed. "You *better*."

God, it was dark out there. I couldn't see a thing. A couple of times, people shot off flares, and while you can't help looking up at them, it messes up your night vision for a few minutes. And anything that makes it harder to see. . . . is a bad thing.

It made good military sense to me that the NVA might hit us that night — why *not* go after a much smaller unit that's reeling from a tough battle? — but I was sure they would wait until later. Three, maybe four, in the morning. When we'd be even more tired, and probably less alert. The skipper says we killed at least 100 NVA out on 881N, and as far as I could tell, there were still hundreds more firing at us. Our company probably went up against a whole battalion, maybe more. But our howitzers, plus the big guns at the main base, had been pounding the jungles for hours now, and maybe that would discourage them.

But those NVA fight hard — you have to give them that.

Right after midnight, we saw a couple of red star cluster flares over Hill 861. That got our attention, since they're right across from our position. Kilo Company mans that hill.

"Those aren't ours, are they?" I asked.

"I don't think so," Bebop said. "Maybe it's —"

We heard the sound of mortar rounds leaving tubes — and then crashing into 861. It seemed to go on and on, and we just stared with our mouths open. It was really weird — like having a front row seat to watch a war.

Gunny Kowalski came by to warn us to stay extra-alert. If the NVA were going after 861, it was a good bet that they were coming here, too. So Bebop and I made ourselves focus on our own lines, gripping our rifles, ready to respond to absolutely *anything*. We had our claymore detonators spread out on a dirt shelf we'd dug near the top of our hole, and a row of grenades lined up, too. We even had elbow holes dug, so we could lean forward and be perfectly steady when we fired our weapons.

Then, the NVA launched a full-out attack on 861. We could hear machine guns, AK-47s, RPGs, grenade explosion, and even high-pitched orders being screamed in Vietnamese. Kilo Company was fighting back, so now we heard American weapons, too. Red and green tracers were zipping back and forth, and it was like watching one of your own worst nightmares come to life.

"Man, those cats are *in* it," Bebop said.

That's for sure. Made me wonder if the guys on 861 had been watching — and listening to — our fight on 881N all afternoon, with the same kind of horror and fascination. Seeing all of the flashes and flares and tracers cut through the darkness was really eerie. I knew men were fighting and dying over there, but I also knew we had to hold *our* hill, no matter what, so we wouldn't be going over to help them. Same reason they hadn't been sent out to help *us*.

Our 81mm mortars were firing a few rounds over to the northwest side of 861, but it wasn't enough to help much. I guess the skipper wanted to keep plenty in reserve in case we needed them to defend ourselves.

The red and green tracers were mixed up all over the top of the hill, which meant that the NVA had broken through and were inside the perimeter. Kilo was *really* in trouble. I couldn't figure out why the NVA wasn't coming up after us, too. We'd know it was starting if any mortar rounds came up here, but so far, nothing.

The battle went on and on — and our hill stayed quiet. Our mortar guys stepped up the pace of their firing, and now we were sending a steady stream of support over to 861. It was pretty amazing — they just sent out hundreds and hundreds of rounds, hour after hour.

Sometime in the middle of the night, Gunny Kowalski came back. He seems old to us, I guess, but this is only his second war. Gunny Sampson — what a good, tough old guy he was — had thought that made Kowalski just a beginner.

"Let's go, boys," he said. "The 81s need us."

It sounded like they were doing just fine on their own, but, okay. Maybe we were going to haul some crates of fresh rounds over to them from the ammo bunker. But that wasn't it, either. They were firing so many rounds, so fast, that the guns were overheating. That's really dangerous, because first, the rounds they fire won't go where they're aimed, and second, the whole thing might melt or blow up on them.

The best way to cool the guns — other than not firing them anymore — is to pour water on them. Except they'd already used all the spare water on the hill. Since no one knew when we'd get resupplied again, the skipper wouldn't let us contribute our canteens to the cause. So, the mortar guys poured all the spare juice they could find on the guns. Sometimes resupply sends us these cans of pretty sour orange, pineapple and grapefruit juice. We drink them, but for some reason, they usually just make you *more* thirsty, so we don't always bother.

The guns were still overheating, and there was only one kind of spare liquid left on the hill. Yep, you got it — every guy on the hill took turns urinating on them. Pretty gross, but it did the trick. The guns were able to keep firing all night long, with the guys singing "The Marines' Hymn" over and over to keep their energy up. But I'm sure not sorry that *I* didn't have to stand next to them for hours.

Between the fire support they were getting, and their own weapons — and guts — Kilo Company drove the last of the NVA out of their perimeter at about five in the morning. When we got the news that Hill 861 was secure, you should have heard the cheers! Our whole hill started shouting at once. Everyone's yelling "Get some!" and "Semper fi!" and all that. It was great to see the good guys win.

In fact — oh, great, here we go again.

Later --

I forgot to mention that for the last couple of days, since the battle, we've started having a bunch of mortar attacks. That was one just now. Snipers are taking shots at us, too. We wear our helmets all the time, and keep our flak jackets fastened all the way up. We did that before, but now we're *serious* about it. We're all just walking targets, so we try to stay in our bunker — or, at least, in the trenches — during the daytime. If they see us come out, they start firing. It's getting crazy.

And I still didn't finish the rest of the story from before. After 861 fought off their attackers, we were all really happy. We heard later that they had only 4 KIAs. Four is still too many, but from watching that insanity? I would have guessed ten times that many guys were killed, if not more. From our perspective, it looked as though the whole company was going to be completely wiped out. They medevaced about 30 guys, and another company got sent out to the hill next to them, 861A, for reinforcements. That way, they'll be able to back each other up.

So, it was heading on to 0530 in the morning, and we were sitting in the fog, eating breakfast. You know you're happy when C rations taste *good*. I plowed through a can of cold chopped ham and eggs in about a minute. Our squad heated up some coffee, opened up cans of peanut butter, jam and crackers — everything was just A-OK in our world.

Then, we heard a funny sound. More than one, actually. Coming from the mountains in the west and zipping straight over our hill. Just as the Professor was saying he thought they might be rockets, we realized that they were heading for the main combat base, KSCB. We'd all been down there, so we knew that most of those guys weren't even dug in. The bunkers were above ground, the mess hall, Charlie Med — it wasn't like the hills, where we *knew* we were a target. We'd been digging in for weeks.

Which doesn't mean that our bunkers couldn't be a lot better, too. But if you don't have any stuff to build overhead cover, what can you do? You just build it up, the best you can. We have lots of long metal stakes that are used for supporting the barbed wire we string around the perimeter. If you put a bunch of them across the top of your bunker, you can cover them with a sheet of plywood or something — if we had plywood; which we don't — and then layer sandbags on top of that. Or we fill empty wooden ammo crates with dirt, and pile them up there. But the stakes really won't hold very much weight, so it's risky. When it comes to overhead cover, the top priority on the hill is to protect our ammo bunkers. If a rocket or artillery shell ever hits one of *them*, the explosion might take the whole rest of the hill along with it.

More rockets were shooting right over us, and mortar and artillery rounds were being fired, too. We couldn't see KSCB too well through the fog, but we knew they were getting hit. Then we heard a huge explosion down there, followed by smaller, secondary explosions.

"Must've gotten the ammo dump," Mooch said.

As we heard more and more explosions at odd intervals — not including the continuing stream of rockets and mortars — I knew he was right. That ammo dump, with literally tons of different ammunition stored there, must have taken a direct hit. Now the guys down there were not only under attack, but their own ammo dump was in danger of killing them, too.

We were all ordered back on alert, just in case the NVA were planning to widen their attack. We could hear small arms fire, machine guns, and mortars off to the south, too. That meant they were either going after the Special Forces camp at Lang Vei, or Khe Sanh Village itself, where the Provincial Headquarters and most of the civilians in the area were.

It was too hard to keep count, but about a hundred mortar rounds must have hit the main base during the first hour alone, with almost as many rockets flying in there, too. With the fog, we were really only able to follow the attack with our ears. Our arty and mortar guys were firing some rounds out towards Laos and 881N, but it was impossible to know where the North Vietnamese were located. We really couldn't see anything, and the mountains and hills absorbed the sounds so that they echoed in a confusing way. Later that morning, there was an explosion at KSCB so intense that *our* hill, four miles away, actually shuddered from the concussion.

"What was *that*?" Bebop asked.

I had absolutely no idea, but it must have been something *big*.

When the fog finally began lifting at about 1200, the main base looked as though it had been *destroyed*. The airstrip was damaged, and most of the above-ground buildings and tents had been pulverized. Black smoke hung over the base, and we could see fires everywhere, especially near the airstrip. The smell of gasoline and burning fuel was really strong, too. We could see the same sort of damage down around Khe Sanh Village — and Hill 861 also looked pretty bad.

I think we forgot that it was risky to be standing outside without the fog to protect us, because when we suddenly got hit with a volley of rockets, a lot of us were caught right out in the open. The NVA must have had our entire position zeroed in, because I think about half a dozen 120mm rounds landed inside our perimeter. Could have been 122mms — I'm not sure. But they both have a *huge* fragmentation radius, so if you're not under cover, you don't even have to be all that close to them to get seriously hurt by all the hot metal shards flying around in the air.

Everyone was diving for cover inside the trenches and our bunkers, but one of the bunkers took a direct hit, which wounded three guys. Two more got riddled with shrapnel from one of the other rounds, which caught them halfway across the saddle, running at top speed. My whole squad raced out there to help move them safely into trenches, so the corpsmen could work on them. The guy Bebop and I carried was all messed up, but we lied and told him he looked okay. The worst part was that most of the damage seemed to be right around his groin. That's the injury that scares us all the most. No one wants to get hurt, but we *really* don't want to get hurt down there.

A medevac was called in right away. The chopper came sooner than I would have expected, since I figured all of the dust-offs must have been flying missions *nonstop* for the past few hours. The helicopter hovered over the landing zone and just as it touched down, the NVA fired a quick volley of mortars right in on top of it. A corpsman and one of the guys guiding the helicopter in were killed instantly, and we had eight or ten more guys badly wounded. The chopper took a bunch of hits, too, and it crash-landed just outside the perimeter. The co-pilot died in the crash, but the rest of the crew was able to scramble up the hill and inside our lines. It was just really — screwed up.

When two more choppers came out to evacuate the casualties, our howitzers and mortars were firing out into the mountains to try and knock out the NVA guns. The skipper called in an artillery barrage from the main base, too. Plus, everyone who hadn't volunteered to carry stretchers was on the line, firing their weapons out at the hills. I'm not sure if it did any good, but we had to try.

Nobody wanted to go back out onto that LZ, but we didn't have much choice — we had to get our people onto the medevac. Most of them were too badly injured to walk. Pugsley and I carried one of the stretchers and shoved the poor guy up into the first helicopter as fast as we could. Then we ran for the trenches, just in case. The chopper was able to take off before any more rockets came in, and the second one came in and out almost as quickly. The whole operation only took a few minutes, and the next round of rockets landed about thirty seconds too late to catch any of us on the landing zone.

Lying down in the trench, trying to make myself as small as possible, all I could think was that there was no way that these trenches could possibly be deep enough to really protect us. I just wanted to start *living* underground from now on.

So, in the space of less than an hour, we had lost another fifteen or twenty people.

Like I said before, suddenly we had a *war* going.

God help us.

January 24, 1968

An NVA soldier walked up to the perimeter today and surrendered. He was lucky that no one shot him, because it was really a shock to have him just show up like that. Especially since we've been taking so many casualties and spending so much time on alert that none of us are getting any sleep. It's hard to think clearly when you're so freakin' tired.

Once the guy was inside our lines, the executive officer from the command post went over to interrogate him. A couple of jets happened to fly by, on a bombing mission, and the NVA guy fell apart. No one ever touched him, but Tiger, one of the RTOs, told me that the guy started crying and everything. Apparently, he was a complete wreck. Looks like all of those bombing missions are having an effect, after all.

Then, when some artillery happened to be fired nearby, he was on the ground, shaking like crazy and babbling to himself. Tiger says it was just pathetic. After that, I guess there wasn't much point in trying to interrogate him. So a chopper came in to take him to the rear, where the intelligence team will probably have a crack at him. A bunch of anti-aircraft fire hit the chopper on the way out, but even though we could see smoke coming from the engine, it kept flying, so I think they made it. Hope so, anyway.

Part of me was glad to hear that the NVA soldier was so screwed up, since they've been hitting us so hard lately — but, another part of me felt sorry for the guy.

I hate to admit it, but mostly, I was glad.

● ● ● ● ● ● ● ● ● ●

January 29, 1968

Man, my coach would flip if he saw me smoking ciga-rettes. But I'm doing it. A lot. So is Bebop. We might be new to smoking — but we're fast learners. I don't even care if it's bad for me. Being in a *war* is bad for me.

Someone on the hill gets hit just about every day. Sometimes, it's not too serious. Sometimes, the guy gets killed. Sometimes, more than one of us gets hit. There's a sniper out somewhere on 881N who might just be the best shot in the world. If you're dumb enough to be walk-ing around in the daylight, and he feels like zapping you — you're gone. Everybody calls him "Luke the Gook." I never used to use that word, but I do now. Just feel like it, I guess. The skipper can call in artillery, order an air strike, have napalm carpet the whole area — and Luke the Gook will pop up five minutes later and start picking us off again. We all hate him.

Most of the time, the mortar and rocket attacks come in during the day — although you can't count on it. We get hit at night, too. Usually, it's a fast volley of five or six rounds, but other times, one will land, and then they'll walk a whole series of rounds right across the hill. You can't outrun them, so you just have to hope that you get lucky and they miss you.

It's all about luck. Or *no* luck. Nobody's happy about it, but nobody's crying, either. It is what it is, that's all.

Our bunkers are no good. Not if you want to live through this. Not that even ten or twelve layers of sandbags would do much good if a rocket makes a direct hit on your position. If that happens, just say your prayers — and say good-bye.

Naturally, they still won't send us up any decent building materials. They don't even send us enough food, or water. And forget about mail; they sure have. It's not safe to go out to the latrines, so we're using empty artillery round cannisters inside our bunkers. Once they're full, you seal them up, and throw them into a special garbage dump set aside for that. Which worked fine, until a mortar round hit directly on top of those cannisters the other day.

Vietnam sucks.

January 31, 1968

The whole country's gone crazy. There was supposed to be a truce for the Tet holiday, and what we're hearing is that they attacked cities and rear areas all over the country last night. Nothing was different here — just the same artillery, mortars, rockets, and sniper rounds. Guys getting hurt, guys dying. You can't help wondering if this war is just spinning out of control.

For us, it's turning into World War I. We live in our trenches, and more and more, we're moving underground. We've had to create a whole new routine. At night, and early in the morning, if it's foggy enough, we can walk around and do whatever we need to do. Fill sandbags, improve our positions, go collect more ammo, check and repair our perimeter defenses and string new comm wire for the radios. But if the sun comes out, or there's any kind of visibility, we don't leave the trenches unless it's absolutely necessary.

Since we've all seen too many bunkers taking direct hits by now, it was time to come up with another form of shelter. So what we're doing is digging "bunny holes." First, we were just digging little shallow holes in the sides of the trenches where we could take cover during rocket and mortar attacks. It's an old infantry strategy, and they're called "roll-outs," because you can just roll right into them in about half a second.

But then someone got the bright idea to make our roll-outs *bigger*. You have to dig carefully, so that tons of dirt don't collapse down on top of you. But if you do it right, you can make nice, safe holes where you can actually get a little sleep during the day. And as time passes, we're making them large enough so that we can pretty much live in them. I guess they look like human-sized burrows or gopher holes, but we call them bunny holes.

So far, the holes are working out okay. That far underground you can take a direct hit, and still have a good chance of surviving. They're really dark, but we use flashlights or candles, if we can scrounge them from other guys. If not, you can actually *make* a crummy little candle out of C ration peanut butter. You roll up a little piece of cloth for a wick, stick it in the peanut butter, and light up. Because of the oil, it'll actually burn for a while, and give off enough light so that you can write letters and play cards and stuff.

We still send out LPs every night, but we aren't doing any patrolling. For one thing, there are so many air strikes every day that if we left the hill, we'd probably get killed by our own bombs. For another, it's absolutely vital that we keep this position secure. If the NVA could run us off here, they would have a perfect view of the main base and could blow it all to pieces whenever they wanted. As long as we're up here, we can make it a little harder for them. Our job is to be "the eyes and ears of Khe Sanh." When we hear the little pops of rockets and mortars being fired, we have fifteen or twenty seconds to warn the main base that they're on their way. There's always a guy posted with a radio to call it down to them, so they can turn on the alert sirens right away. Maybe it saves some lives. Can't hurt, anyway.

When the weather's clear enough, there are air strikes and bombing missions all day long. Someone told me it's called Operation Niagra, because the bombs just keep falling in a stream that never stops.

The B-52 strikes are just awesome. Their bombing missions are called Arc Lights. The B-52s are huge jets which fly so high that you usually can't see them or hear them. But then, out of nowhere, the ground starts shaking underneath you and some huge portion of the jungle —

maybe a quarter of a mile or more — just blows up. Those bombs land miles away, and the force is still strong enough to bounce us right up off the ground here on the hill. The first time I saw one, the explosions were so massive and bright that I honestly thought President Johnson had lost his mind and decided to use nuclear weapons. The flash from the bombs was really blinding, and I was sure that we were all going to die from the radiation. I felt stupid when the Professor told me they were only bombs. Just really *big* bombs.

I can't imagine what it would be like to be out there when one of those B-52 strikes hits the ground. Everything nearby disintegrates, and you don't have any warning at all that it's even coming. Your world just suddenly disappears. I'm glad I'm not NVA; it must be completely terrifying to be on the receiving end of all those air strikes. The truth is, anyone who can fight through that without falling apart is someone whose hand I want to shake. A guy like that is damned tough.

The main base gets hit with mortars and rockets, on and off, all day, every day. By now, I assume they must just stay underground, too. And if they don't — they're morons. But as far as we can tell from here, they have trenches and everything now. Forget Khe Sanh; the whole place should just be called Sandbag City.

I wish the NVA would just attack us, and be done with it. What are they waiting for? Or, better yet, I wish we'd get sent out there to *find* them. You want guys to sit around like lumps all day and be target practice for the enemy, why not bring the Army up here? You shouldn't waste Marines in defensive positions. We're a *fighting* force, not a sit-around-and-get-picked-off-one-by-one force. Seems like a real waste of resources, to me.

Not that anyone asked.

I haven't been writing any letters lately, because I can't think of anything to say that wouldn't sound bad. Besides, we're not getting too many chances to send mail out. Three choppers have already been shot down around the hill, so I don't guess those pilots like coming out here much. Especially not when it's just to pick up mail. I should write some, anyway.

Of course, I could also try to get some sleep.

Yeah. Sleep sounds good.

February 5, 1968

Hill 861A almost got overrun last night. I thought we might be attacked, too, because we took a lot more mortar rounds than usual, and even some rockets. But we fired missions of our own, and on the lines, we threw grenades at every single sound we heard out past the perimeter. Before the night was over, we all had another long session of lining up to help the mortar guys "cool down" their guns. Right before I left, my father said, "do what you have to do." He was definitely right about that one. Live in dirt holes, go without food and water, wear the same clothes for weeks, fire your weapon at complete strangers and try to kill them. So, that's what I do. At this point, I just want to survive long enough to make it back home.

The only reason I haven't lost it is the other guys. If one of us gets down, the rest of us pick him up. We try to, anyway. And when you're crammed into such close quarters, you'd *better* get along. But that makes it worse when you lose a guy. I didn't know him that well, but Twerp got hit yesterday and I feel lousy about it. He was a nice kid, really into cars, always carried these ragged old issues of *Popular Mechanics* around. He was going down the line to see some of his buddies in the second squad and got taken out by a 120mm mortar round. We got him onto a medevac, but he had a really bad head wound, so I doubt that he made it.

Which stinks.

It stinks more that the two helicopter support guys who were guiding the chopper in got caught by a mortar the NVA fired onto the LZ. It was five hours before another medevac came in to get them, and one of them was in such bad shape that he spent most of that time screaming.

In the last few days, we got about eight new replacements, and half of them have already been medevaced out. One of them didn't even make it off the chopper. Because he was a new guy, he didn't know that you *have* to keep your flak jacket zipped and fastened all the way up, so he got the full force of the blast right in the chest. It was really terrible. We just had to wrap him in a poncho, and leave him near the LZ. Medevacs will only come in for emergency cases now, and sometimes priority cases. KIAs are considered routine.

The new lieutenant who came in with the replacements took it really hard. I guess he had different ideas about what being in a war zone was like. No wonder salts always just give new guys that grim grin and say, "Welcome to the war, boot!"

Bebop and I were lying in our bunny hole this morning and splitting a can of fruit cocktail. We're so short on food and water right now that everything is being strictly rationed, so we always share. We get about half a canteen to drink every day — if we're lucky enough to get that much. Anyway, we were just lying around in there, waiting for the latest mortar attack to end. I had my arm over my eyes, because every time a round hit too close, dirt would come showering down into my face. We had our boots off, because the skipper wants us to air our feet out whenever we can, to protect against getting trench foot. I don't even want to describe how my feet look after wearing the same boots — and socks — for weeks on end. And my head itches all the time, so I'm afraid I might have lice or something.

"You know, Mighty Mouse," Bebop said, sounding very serious. "Vietnam just really isn't good for your health."

I know it's not funny — but I laughed my head off. Just something about the way he said it, I guess.

Being in Vietnam? Unhealthy? Go figure.

February 8, 1968

We lost Lang Vei last night. From up here, we could see — and hear — most of it. I think the main base was supposed to send reinforcements out to them, but we never heard any choppers or anything heading that way. And the jungle's too thick between them and the base for any infantry to be able to *walk* it in enough time to help out.

The same's true for us on the hill. If we ever get attacked, we're on our own. No one talks about it — but we all know that we've been written off before it even happens.

I don't know how many of those Special Forces guys and CIDG troops (mostly Montagnards) survived — but the scuttlebutt around here is that more than half of them were killed. The civilians around there must have been caught up in it, too. Can you *imagine* someone fighting a war right in the middle of your hometown? Maybe we *are* doing the right thing, by being here and trying to help get the NVA out of here.

Or maybe we're just making it worse. If we *weren't* here, the NVA might just leave all of those poor people alone. I don't know — I don't really understand any of it. Before I got here, I just assumed that the generals and the government knew what they were doing. But now that I'm right in the middle of it? None of this makes any sense. We lose at least one guy almost every single day on this hill — and, for what?

If I thought we were actually accomplishing something, okay. But — I don't see it. The Professor says we're just cannon fodder while the White House hopes that Hanoi gets tired of all this and goes away. Hanoi is waiting for the same thing. In the meantime, lots of big defense contractors make a bunch of money building weapons that don't work right, military officers get to award themselves a bunch of medals and get promoted a lot, and back at home, most people are just sitting around watching *Bonanza* and complaining that their taxes are too high.

Wish I didn't agree with him.

But I do.

February 9, 1968

A lot of guys were feeling really down today, because two of our gunny sergeants got killed today. One mortar took out both of them. They did everything right — heard the pop, ducked, and ran for the nearest hole, but a round landed right on top of them. Nothing you can do to prevent it. Bad luck, Vietnam-style. Those two men had more time combined in the Marines than most of the rest of us put together, so I guess that makes us all feel extra shook-up about it. And the cloud cover is so heavy that no one's even going to fly up here to take them away today. Maybe tomorrow, they said. Or the next day. If nothing more important comes up in the meantime.

Shows the respect you get for devoting your whole adult life to serving your country.

All I want to do is go home — and I've got eleven months to go.

February 11, 1968

Bad day. Even worse than usual.

Mooch took a sniper's bullet in the stomach yesterday. He had his flak jacket on, but they only protect us from shrapnel. It was a really serious wound, but the new corpsman said he'd be okay if we could get him evacuated right away.

And then, the fog rolled in, as thick as I'd ever seen it. All of the helicopters were grounded again, and we had no way of getting him out until the weather cleared. So the corpsman, Doc Jarvis, had to try and keep him alive for however long it took to get the medevac in. Food and water aren't the only things that are scarce up here — we're also always close to running out of bandages, glucose, blood expanders, and all the other stuff the corpsmen need.

We all knew it was bad. I think Mooch knew, too, but he never said so. We were on alert, because the NVA were probing our lines on and off all night, so we had to take turns sitting with him. The only time he complained was to say how thirsty he was. Doc Jarvis told us that people with stomach wounds aren't supposed to drink anything, and just to try and change the subject whenever he asked.

Not that we have any damn water up here, anyway — although we would have given Mooch every bit of it. At this point, we have ponchos strung up all the place, because when the dew and mist gather on the plastic, we can collect a little water. Not much, but when they talk about beggars not being choosers? We've all turned into beggars.

It was about three in the morning, and I was sitting next to Mooch in the section of trench we were using as an aid station. He was lying on the ground on a thick layer of poncho liners, because we were trying to make him comfortable. Every so often, we could hear a bunch of grenades go off, or a little flurry of automatic weapons fire — theirs *and* ours.

"You should be on the sixty, man," Mooch said. His voice had gotten all raspy and weak, by now. He slurred most of his words, too.

I shook my head, and told him it gave Bebop a chance to feel rough and tough. He actually does love firing the pig; he just doesn't want to have to carry it around. Who does? It weighs more than twenty pounds — and that doesn't include the ammunition, the extra barrels, the tripod, and everything else you have to bring along with it.

Even with artillery firing and air strikes and all of the other noise going on outside, it seemed quiet where we were. I had leaned an M-16 against the trench wall, in case the hill was assaulted and I needed to protect us.

"Can't feel my legs, man," Mooch said, very matter of fact.

Doc Jarvis was pretty sure the bullet had bounced around inside him, and was probably resting against his spinal cord. Or, it might have done even more damage than that — Doc just didn't know.

"Well, we'll get you out of here really soon, and the docs at Charlie Med will fix you right up," I said. I hope I *sounded* like I believed it. It was hard to tell whether Mooch wanted to talk, or just be quiet together, so I was trying my best to follow his cues.

He didn't say anything for a few minutes, and I was afraid he had passed out — or worse.

"What are you always writing in that blue book?" he wanted.

You know, no one had ever asked me that before — not even Bebop. "Just the stuff that happens here," I said. "What I think about it. I don't know."

"Are you good at writing?" he asked.

I told him the truth, which is that no, I'm not, and I pretty much use the same words over and over, because I don't know very many. But he asked me if I would help him write letters to his mother and his wife, and of course, I said yes. Since we haven't gotten any mail for so long, none of us knows how are our families are doing, or what's happening back in the world. With choppers getting shot down and crashing all the time, we don't even know if *our* letters are getting to *them*.

Anyway, Doc Jarvis gave me a pen and some paper.

Both of Mooch's letters were sweet, and simple, and full of love. That he was okay, that he didn't want them to worry, but he just wanted them to know how he felt about them. I think I almost started crying when he had me tell his wife that if anything happened to him, he wanted her to find someone else. That she was too young to be alone, and whoever she married was going to be the second luckiest guy on earth.

As we wrote, his voice was getting weaker and it seemed to be an effort for him to breathe. I kept asking if he wanted to stop for a while, and he'd say, "Nope, gotta do this *now*."

"You think those'll be okay?" he asked, when we were finished with the letters, and I was addressing the envelopes. "That they'll like them?"

"I think they'll love them," I said. *Treasure* them.

Mooch died just after 0930 this morning. He was seventeen years old.

The fog lifted maybe twenty minutes later.

February 14, 1968

I don't want to make any more friends. It's just too hard. Bebop and the Professor are the only two guys left in the squad from when I first got in-country. Pugsley's the only other old guy. We're getting a lot of new replacements, but it seems like most of them don't even make it a week out here before they get hit. So, what's the point of making friends with them? The more friends you have, the more depressing it is, because you keep losing them all the time.

But I remember when I got here, and no one talked to me for the first week. So I don't like turning right around and doing that to other people. Guess I can't win, no matter what I do.

Seems like there's a lot of that going around here lately.

Morale is pretty low — the worst I've seen it. So, the skipper has started holding flag ceremonies at 0800 in the morning, and then again at sundown. At first, I thought it was the stupidest thing I ever heard. All of us, standing out in the open, at attention, saluting — while the NVA drop mortars on top of our heads? Yeah, great idea.

But, you know, it's actually turned out to be okay. From the time we hear the little pop — depending on the kind of mortar, sometimes it's more like a "*boop*" or a "*thunk*" — we have just over twenty seconds to get out of the way. That's *plenty* of time to find your way into a trench or something. One of the new lieutenants even has a bugle. He's not very good, but hey, he plays better than I do. Bebop borrowed it one time, to see how he could do, but said brass just wasn't his thing and gave it back.

Anyway, the lieutenant plays "To the Colors"— really fast — and we all stand at attention while two guys raise the flag. We finish up, leap into the trenches or the CP bunker, and laugh like wild men as the mortar rounds come in. We all take turns raising and lowering the flag, and we dug a couple of deep holes right next to the pole so that the two guys can jump right in, instead of trying to make it to the trenches. At first, we were just using a radio antenna for a flagpole, but now we've rigged up a more permanent one.

When you think about it, it's a great idea. Shows the NVA that we're not at all scared of them. Plus, it gives us something to do that's patriotic, rebellious, and really *dumb*. Kind of the perfect combination for a Marine.

Found out a little while ago that we're not allowed to fly the American flag, without flying the South Vietnamese one, too — but are any of them up here in the dirt with the rest of us? Nope. We're happy to fly their flag; they just have to come on up and help us raise it.

Don't see that happening, somehow. Until then, we'll just get a charge out of looking at the Stars and Stripes flapping around in the fog and clouds.

We're using more than one LZ now, to try and keep the NVA off-balance. We pop different colors of smoke at the last second, and only the chopper pilots know which color is the correct one. So, they land, and the NVA just have to guess where it might be. Sometimes — too often — they guess right, but it helps a little.

The resupply choppers don't even land anymore, unless they're dropping off new replacements or picking up guys who are going on R&R or something. They just cut loose a cargo net of supplies and try to time it so that it lands safely on the LZ. At least half of the time, the plastic water containers — we call them "water bladders" — break open from the force of hitting the ground. Here we are, practically dying of thirst, and you have to sit there and watch water spilling out all over the ground without being able to do anything about it.

Last week, a huge load of ammo and C rations drifted off to one side and crushed two poor guys from Hotel Company. That was just *ugly*. Other times, the supplies miss the hill completely, and land somewhere down the sides of the hill, past the perimeter. When that happens, we're always under orders to blow them up, so that the NVA won't be able to take the stuff for themselves. Everyone gets really mad when that happens, because we're *just sure* that our mail is getting blown up down there, too.

Today, though, one of the choppers had to land, because we were sending out two priority medevacs, and a guy from 1st Platoon whose tour is up. Man, did we all envy *him*. I helped with one of the stretchers, because I happened to be on my way back from the ammo bunker, where I was picking up some extra rounds for the sixty.

A replacement leaped out of the chopper, and made a dash for the trench. He rolled into it, and landed right on top of me. When I saw who it was, I blinked, and then grinned at him.

"Hi, Rotgut," I said, and punched him really hard in the stomach. "Welcome back."

The wind was knocked out of him for a minute, but then he laughed and straightened his glasses. "You owed me that one, hunh?"

Good. He hadn't forgotten about slugging me during the battle on 881N. "Yep," I said. Wow, it was great to see one of the old guys back. "How you doing, buddy?" There was a red raised scar running across his cheek and down his jaw, but other than that, he seemed fine.

"I'm okay," he said, and turned onto his back to look around. The trench was much deeper than it had been when he left, and the bunny-holes and roll-outs were new, too. So were the mortar and artillery attacks, for that matter. "Did I miss anything?"

"Not a thing," I said.

February 19, 1968

Sprained my ankle pretty badly today. Got caught in the open when the mortars started, and landed all wrong inside the nearest trench. Doc Jarvis taped it up for me, and I can walk, but just barely. It's the same ankle I always used to sprain playing basketball, so maybe it's just not as strong as the other one. Hope I don't have to do any serious running the next few days, or I'm in trouble.

After that, we got orders to hunker down inside our holes. Some general somewhere had decided to "experiment" and have a B-52 Arc Light raid fly much closer than usual to our position. I guess they thought they might catch a bunch of NVA by surprise. But they weren't sure if it would be safe to drop those massive bombs that close to friendly positions. So, guess who got to be the guinea pigs? Yep, who else? Hill 881S.

We were supposed to be alerted over the squad radios exactly when the bombs were being dropped. Then — even though they were *sure* nothing would go wrong — they wanted us to cover our ears and yell as loud as we could, to help protect us from the concussion of the bombs.

Well, I'll tell you one thing — when the bombs hit and started bouncing us off the ground and slamming us into the dirt walls — remembering to scream was *not* a problem.

Even after it was over, we all just sat there in a daze, with our mouths hanging open. Most of us had bloody noses — just from the force of the explosions — and I couldn't hear at all out of my left ear. Still can't, actually.

Hope the generals enjoyed the show.

February 23, 1968

The main base really got pounded today. It started early, and didn't let up all day. Had to be at least a thousand rounds, maybe more. I wonder how many people got hurt.

Not that we didn't take a bunch of rounds, too, but what else is new? My ear still doesn't feel right, so I'm wearing my helmet tilted to one side most of the time. That way, I can use my good ear to pick up those god-awful metallic pops when the rounds get dropped into their tubes and head our way. By now, most of us can tell exactly what kind of round it is, and make a pretty good guess of where it's going to land, just by the sound.

I thought about asking for a medevac to go get my ear checked out — but most of the artillery and mortar guys are half-deaf at this stage of the game, and I don't see them going anywhere. So, I won't, either.

My ankle still hurts a lot, too. Just for the record.

This afternoon, a guy from 2nd Platoon suddenly flipped out. We've had a couple of guys wig out so far, but not too many, all things considered. Anyway, he was this big tough redneck named Dixie, who usually swaggered around with a big wad of chewing tobacco stuffed in his cheek, but I guess life on 881S was a little more than he could take. First, he let off a whole magazine inside his bunker. Said he was only trying to kill rats, but the other guy who was in there at the time didn't want to hear it. They got into a fight, but the rest of their squad broke it up pretty quickly.

But then, Dixie came running outside and jumped up on top of a pile of sandbags near the perimeter. He was swearing and waving his arms in the air and yelling for the NVA to just go ahead and send him home, if they were so tough.

The guy got his wish. Some machine gunner out in the hills stitched him right across the chest about ten seconds later.

So he'll be going home. In a bag.

February 25, 1968

The mood on the hill is pretty dark lately. Too much shelling, too many mortar attacks, too many casualties. Not enough food, water, and mail. Nothing new there, but after a while, it really gets to you.

Bebop must have decided that we all needed some big league cheering up, because right after the fog burned off today, he headed down the trench to the saddle between our company and Hotel Company. We use it as one of our LZs, but the NVA have the location so accurately locked in with their weapons, that we call it "No Man's Land."

"What's he doing?" Pugsley asked me.

How was I supposed to know? But I made my way down the trench, too, in case he was about to have a nervous breakdown and dance around like that guy Dixie the other day. People seemed to sense that something was up, and a bunch of guys came yawning out of their bunny holes to see what was going on.

I could see that Bebop was about to climb out of the trench — and I didn't like it.

"Cut it out, man!" I yelled from where I was standing. "It's not funny."

Bebop just grinned at me, took a deep breath, and jumped out onto No Man's Land. Then he spread his arms out to the side and ran across the saddle, singing "The hills are alive, with the sound of mortars!" at the top of his lungs. We all heard the pop of the tubes, but Bebop stopped in the middle of No Man's Land and twirled once. Then he ran the rest of the way across the saddle, still singing his own made-up lyrics to the song, and tumbled into the trench with about three seconds to space.

The mortars came in, right on target, but we were all safely down inside the trenches and bunny holes, and the shrapnel just sprayed around harmlessly. Once the barrage stopped, we all laughed so hard that my stomach still hurts, hours later.

"The twirl, man," the Professor said to Bebop. "The twirl made it beautiful."

Bebop just grinned, and looked at the rest of us. "Who's next?" he asked.

And just like that, we had a new standard for coolness on the hill. You get extra points if the visibility is really good, but because it takes a few extra seconds, for slow runners, the twirl is optional.

Real Marines are proud to imitate Maria Von Trapp.

● ● ● ● ● ● ● ● ● ●

February 27, 1968

This guy the captain's been using as a spotter struck gold today. Saw some movement out near Co Roc Mountain in Laos, and told the skipper he'd located one of the NVA's big guns. It was too far away for our howitzers to hit it, but the skipper got on the horn and brought in some jets cruising nearby. Our spotter managed to put some bombs directly onto the position, and we all cheered when he said the gun had been blown to bits. Far as he could tell, the NVA were storing the gun in some kind of cave. They must roll it out just to pop off a few rounds, and then roll it back in out of sight. Our jets will probably start carpet-bombing that whole location regularly now, and maybe we'll get lucky and they'll take the rest of the artillery pieces and mortars out, too.

Took that guy *two weeks* of staring out there, but he finally got them. Hope they put him in for a medal — he deserves it.

We've also been able to wipe out two snipers recently, using the 106mm recoilless rifles. Those 106mm guys are so used to firing at 881N that they can pretty much pinpoint every shot, if they want. They just need a good target. All we have to do is locate the muzzle flash when the sniper shoots at us, and then the recoilless guys put a round right in there. Since each of those snipers was responsible for hitting about ten of our people apiece — including Mooch, we cheered when the rifles took them out.

The new Luke the Gook is a whole different story. I'm

not sure if the guy could hit you if you stood five feet in front of him. He pops off rounds all day long, but never even comes close. So, we've been having a little fun with old Luke. We hold up targets for him — like a helmet on top of a really long stick, and see if he can hit them. When he misses, we hold up a red flag to let him know, just the way the drill sergeants used to on the rifle range. At boot camp, it was called "Maggie's Drawers." A couple of guys made this flag by nailing a pair of USMC issue swim trunks — red, with some gold markings — to a tent pole. So, when our pal Luke misses, we give him a good old Marine salute. It's always good for a laugh. I wouldn't be surprised if it makes Luke laugh, too.

It's easy to find his muzzle flashes, but we're not going to go after him. If we do, they might find a sniper who can actually *shoot* worth a damn. But we like Luke — he can stay around as long as he wants. Unless his aim starts getting better.

When you get down to it, most of the NVA are probably just guys like us — who happen to be Vietnamese. But, a grunt is a grunt, I figure. We do all the dirty work, while a bunch of politicians and generals sit around in air-conditioned offices and make up really dumb plans. For all I know, their civilians back in Hanoi even whine that they're jerks for serving their country.

We actually got *mail* today. Second time this week. Division finally figured out a resupply plan that works. It's called "Super Gaggle," and it's pretty impressive. Instead of sending choppers out here all by their lonesome, now they have escorts. *Lots* of escorts.

First, some jets come swooping in and drop bombs and napalm. A couple more jets follow that with cannisters of tear gas, and two more are right on their trail dropping smoke to screen the NVA's view of our hill. Then, as more jets release another load of bombs, a bunch of CH-46 helicopters come flying in to the hill to bring in our supplies and — too often — take out casualties. They're escorted by Huey gunships, helicopters that shoot up the whole area with rockets, and machine gun fire from their door-gunners. We call that "strafing."

And, hey, just so we don't feel left out, the helicopter support teams up here throw more smoke on the LZs, while the rest of us fire off a couple of magazines apiece. In my case, I blast through two or three belts of ammo, hosing down the terrain in front of me, while the other machine gunners do the same.

Do we still get mortared during all of this? Well, yeah, more often than not. But, a lot more supplies are getting through now.

Can't tell you how great it is to have *mail*. I got 14 letters, and a small package of stuff from my family. One of the letters from my mother asked me if I liked the dictionary she sent — which must have been in one of the cargo loads that landed outside the perimeter during the last few weeks.

One of the ones we had to blow up. Unless some NVA guy snuck in and got there first, and is sitting in his foxhole right now, expanding his vocabulary and all.

Jackson, who's been here — well, I forget how long — got a box of chocolate chip cookies from his grandmother, plus two cans of cashew nuts and some Vienna sausages. So, *he's* pretty popular at the moment. Rotgut is, too, because he got two cartons of cigarettes and a plastic container full of whiskey from some guy he knows stationed down at Long Binh.

From my family's letters, I can tell that most—if not all — of my mail is getting through. So they know that I'm okay. They're really worried about me being "under siege." Khe Sanh is a huge story back in the States, apparently. Front page headlines, magazine cover stories, Walter Cronkite broadcasting about us every night. *Under siege?* Man, that stinks. Makes it sound like we're all crying and hiding and ready to surrender — when instead, we're chomping (champing? Hell, I don't know) at the bit to get out there and take the NVA on, face-to-face. I don't call that a *siege*. Leave sieges for the boys at the Alamo — not the *Marines*.

All of which I plan to write back to them, in a long, gung-ho letter.

"We're under siege," I told the Professor, who was sitting next to me in the trench. We were just outside our bunny holes, so we'd have enough light to read.

"I know," he said, and indicated the letters he was reading from *his* family. "I heard."

Molly sent me Audrey's address off at college — so I owe her one. So far, I can handle all of this war stuff, but, okay, the thought of sending Audrey a letter makes me a little nervous. I'll have to think about that. I wonder if she's turned into an I-Hate-the-War hippie, and marches around carrying signs and all. I also wonder if Keith is still in the picture. But, I could still write her, and just say hi. How hard would *that* be?

Pretty hard.

Pugsley must have written home about how cold and damp it gets up here, especially at night. Because his mother sent him a brand-new slicker. The funny part? It's *bright-orange.*

"Put it on, then turn around so I can draw a big old target sign on your back," Bebop suggested.

The sweet part is that you know his mother really meant well, and would be horrified if she realized her son would be in terrible danger if he ever wore it. Pugsley just shrugged and said he's going to use it to decorate the inside of his bunny hole. It'll definitely brighten the place up! We'll need sunglasses in there.

I saved my package for last, because I knew it would be the most fun. My family had sent me a bunch of Kool-Aid packets, some iced tea mix, half-melted Milky Way bars, a few articles about the Red Sox getting ready for spring training, a deck of cards, more pens and paper, a pair of socks, and some raisins. When I took out the socks, everybody nearby looked at me and I felt really guilty that there was only one pair. Makes it really hard to share.

"Swap you your socks for my new jacket," Pugsley said.

Oh, yeah. *That's* gonna happen.

"I could maybe just wear one, and someone else could have the other," I said, even though it was a pretty dumb idea.

"Take off your boots," Rotgut said. "Let's see how bad they are."

Like almost everyone else, my feet are really disgusting and I have some rotten kind of fungus growing all over them. I guess it's what they call immersion foot. My boots were already unlaced — since we weren't planning on leaving the trenches until it got dark — and I pulled the right one off to show my half-rotten, full of holes sock.

"Keep them socks for you'self," Tyler, who's a high school drop-out from West Virginia, said.

Even though Tyler's a new guy, everyone else seemed to agree with him. So, I put on my new socks before any of them changed their minds. I was about to throw the grungy old ones up out of the trench, but Bebop stopped me.

"Leave them near our hole," he said. "I think the smell might kill the rats."

Like his smelled any better? But I grinned and dropped the filthy socks in the dirt.

Man, talk about luxury. *New socks.*

February 29, 1968

Wouldn't it just *figure* that this would be a leap year? That means, like it or not, we all have to serve an extra day on our tours.

Terrific.

March 3, 1968

It's really late, and I've been guarding the line all night. Bebop has some pretty bad dysentery, so I've been letting him get some extra sleep. He did the same for me, a few nights ago, when I had a terrible headache. Anyway, I decided I'd write a few paragraphs, just to try and stay awake. I probably won't be able to read any of this later, since it's so dark — but I don't have enough water to make coffee, and I have to find a way to stay alert.

We had some noise out on the wire before. Another probe, I guess. Unless it was rock apes — there are a lot of them in the jungle around here. One of them actually came right through the perimeter once. Scared the guy who saw him so much that the kid almost passed out before firing a whole magazine at him. People laughed pretty hard about it the next day because even with all of those bullets at short-range, he *missed*. No dead rock ape in front of his position. Not even any *blood* out there. If the guy in the next hole hadn't seen the whole thing, I would have figured that the kid was making it all up. But I'd be really scared, too, if some huge, furry thing on two legs decided to lurch right up to me in the middle of the night.

Resupply sends us so many grenades, that we throw them if we even *think* we hear someone out there. Most of us have about a case apiece stored in our bunkers. If you shoot, you just give away your position, because of the muzzle flashes and tracer rounds. And with me on the M-60 these days, they'd be aiming at *me*, first. So I'm glad the skipper lets us use grenades whenever we're in doubt. (Okay, and sometimes when we're just *bored*.)

I never get used to standing guard by myself at night. I know I'm not alone, but it sure feels that way. And I've *seen* the other hills get attacked, so there's no reason why they won't decide to overrun us some night. I know we'd fight until the last man, but they could definitely "put a hurt on us," like the guys always say.

The B-52s fly night sorties, as well as the day missions, and it's always a shock when some ridge out in front of you erupts into flames unexpectedly. The fast movers streak by, too, but at least you can see and hear them coming, so you know that more bombs are about to explode out there.

My favorite to watch is Puff the Magic Dragon. Puffs are these old AC-47 gunships, outfitted with Gatling guns. Some people call them "Spooky," but I like "Puff." Everyone says they can fill a whole football field with lead in about a minute. I don't like to think of bullets and football fields in the same sentence, but Puff's firepower is really something. It can fire one hundred rounds *a second*.

Even though only every fifth round is a tracer, you just see this endless stream of red drifting down to the ground. It looks so pretty that you forget that you're watching bullets being fired. Instead, it's just Puff, painting red streaks across the sky.

Even when it's pitch black or fogged out, NVA snipers and machine gunners still fire at us at night. Talk about a shot in the dark. But it's scary when you hear those .51 caliber rounds go buzzing by, or see green tracers heading towards the hill. Our howitzers or the recoilless rifles usually pump a few answering rounds out there, but unless there's a secondary explosion in the hills — from striking an NVA ammo cache or something — there's no way of knowing whether they hit anything.

And, even though it makes sense logically, I can't figure out why both sides use different colored tracers. Seems too civilized. Should a war really be *logical* like that? I'd rather throw a few green tracers out there sometimes, try to fake the NVA out.

I keep waiting for some commander to ask me my opinion about stuff like this, but so far, no dice. For the people in charge back in Washington, I think this is all one big war game to them. *They're* not the ones watching their friends lying on the LZ in ponchos or body bags, while we wait a couple of days for a chopper to come pick up these "routine" medevacs.

Must be fun to run a war when you don't actually have to *fight* in it.

March 9, 1968

I'm really homesick today. It's my little sister's birthday, and I'm not there. I wrote her a long birthday letter the other week, but it's not like I could get her a decent present — or really any present at all. The Professor's parents developed a bunch of rolls of film he sent home and mailed them back, so he let me have a good one of me goofing around with Bebop, Pugsley, and Perez, and I stuck it in her birthday envelope. I mean, what else do I have to send her — a can of C rat peanut butter? A bottle of bug juice? Cigarettes? Some bullets? You know, it feels like Perez was evacuated out of here years ago, but I'm not sure it's been even two months. Things are so intense over here that time gets confusing.

Anyway, she's turning sixteen, so it's a big one.

Oh, *here's* a horrible thought — Molly, behind the wheel. Boston had better look out for her. Knowing Molly, she'll bring a book along to read at red lights. At least, I hope it's only at red lights.

I bet it'll be a great party, though. Mom'll bake a huge layer cake — probably chocolate with vanilla frosting. Roast chicken, mashed potatoes, carrots, beets — which only Molly and my mother even like. Brenda will probably bake bread and bring the kids over, and Hank will come, too, if he's not working. Some aunts and uncles and cousins will probably stop by. Molly will definitely invite her friend Theresa, and probably a couple of other friends. And whenever there's a party, you can count on a few firefighters to show up.

But you know that *this* time, Dad's going to be watching like a hawk to make sure none of them starts making a move on her, since Brenda and Hank met when *she* was sixteen. If I was there, I'd go up to Dad every so often, and say, "Watch out, Fitzy was just holding her hand!" and stuff like that. I'd probably be able to get away with it at least twice before he figured out that I was just pulling his leg.

My parents were a little mad at me on my birthday last summer, because I went marching off downtown first thing in the morning, to sign up at the USMC recruiting station. They knew I was going to do it — but they weren't that happy. I think they were proud, though — or, anyway, my father was. Secretly. My mother was just worried.

We're all so hungry that we spend hours talking about food up here. I think we talk more about food than we do girls — which only goes to show that we are *not* in our right minds.

Girls come in a close second, though — no contest. In fact, I got my nerve up and wrote Audrey a letter today. I couldn't think of much to put in it, but at least I said hi. Told her where I was, what I was doing — and that I really wished that before we graduated, I'd told her that I thought she was cool. I kept it pretty short, so that if she doesn't write back, it won't bother me as much. But I hope she —

Just looked at my watch, and it's almost time for me to go take my time on OP. Observation posts are just like LPs, except they take place during the day, and you're usually out there alone — with a pair of binoculars, if you're lucky. I'm going to be on the east side of the hill today, out past the perimeter. It's one of the most dangerous things we have to do around here, since we're really exposed out there, if the weather is clear.

Like today.

Can't wait.

March 14, 1968

Shadow came back to the unit from the hospital today — and never made it off the LZ. I was asleep in my bunny hole and didn't actually see him, but Pugsley told me about it later. Three of our artillery guys were being medevaced — one of the howitzers took a direct hit this morning, and only one of the guys in the gun pit managed to get out of the way in time. A CH-46 was already heading in with a few new replacements, including Shadow, so they were going to take out the WIAs, too.

Pugsley says Shadow ran out of the helicopter, but then stopped to help get one of the makeshift stretchers — we keep running out of real ones and they won't send us more — inside. His reward? A round through the shoulder, that nearly took his arm off. The crew chief yanked him back into the chopper, and they left.

Almost two months in the hospital from the 881N battle, and Shadow didn't even last back on the hill for a full minute.

I hope he's going to be okay.

March 17, 1968

It's St. Patrick's Day today, which I think of as being my own personal holiday. Irish on both sides of the family, on top of being named for the guy? We both even hate snakes.

Wonder how he felt about rats.

At least I'm wearing green. I *think* my uniform's still green, under all of the dirt. It's also possible that my skin isn't actually made of red clay — but you couldn't prove it by looking at me. At any of us. When replacements show up, their skin — black, white, anything in-between — looks so *bright* and shiny. Until they start to get grungy like us, they really stick out.

Regiment Command let us have a little fun today, though, because every unit was authorized to fire off all of their green smoke. I threw about six green smoke grenades myself, since everyone kept giving them to me and the other Irish guys. Amazing how many of us there are here — we've got McCarthys, O'Reillys, and Callahans coming out of our ears. (Just to name a few.) And you'll never meet *anyone* Irish — at least I never have — who isn't totally proud of it.

Which reminds me. One of my buddies from high school, Eddie Finnegan, is over here, too. We were on the baseball team together, and he was the scrappiest kid you'd ever want to meet. No catchers blocked the plate when *Eddie* came sliding in. Broke up double plays right and left, too. Picked fights, too, in the parking lot afterwards.

Some other guys from my school have either joined up, or already gotten back to the World, if they were a grade or two ahead of me. And — yeah — a couple didn't make it home. Brighton High School is definitely doing its share, but I think Eddie's the only other guy who's also in-country right now. I don't have his address, but last I heard, he was down near Chu Lai, with the Americal. So, he's a doggie, but in this one case, I'll let that pass. Odds are, he's a *good* doggie.

I'm going to have to ask my mother if she can get his address for me — she and Mrs. Finnegan are both in the St. Anthony's Rosary & Altar Society and everything. It'd be nice to write to a guy who would really understand what I was talking about — and who I've known since I was little. I guess with its being St. Patrick's Day, I automatically started thinking about him.

Wonder what kind of war *he's* having.

March 23, 1968

I can't believe it. I got hit. It's not even that bad, but they still made me go down to Charlie Med at the main base. Probably because I was knocked out for a couple of minutes, and that made Doc Jarvis worry.

I guess I should be glad it happened when I was doing my job, not just skylarking. I pulled a really crummy detail today — bodyguard duty. We have these two forward observers stationed up on the hill who work for tactical air control and spot targets of opportunity for the jets and artillery and gunships to hit. Because they have to concentrate on what they're doing, the shipper assigns a grunt to each of them for protection. While the FOs peer out at the jungle and the hills through their binoculars, we're supposed to make sure they don't get hurt. So, we stay on watch, and if mortars start coming in or something, we hustle them over to a trench. If there isn't enough time to get out of the way, we're under orders to knock them down and cover them with our bodies so that they won't get hit with any shrapnel.

Could be just me, but no one seems too worried about *us* getting hit with shrapnel.

It's not such bad duty when it's foggy, but the weather has been much more clear the last couple of weeks. So, the FOs have even more missions to call in than usual, but they're also better targets for the NVA. We try to keep them near decent cover, but since they're balancing a radio, maps, and their binoculars all at the same time, they tend to get really distracted. Being an FO is a hard job, though — takes a lot more patience than I have.

So we're hunkered down on the edge of the hill, me with an M-16 — which feels even more like a toy than it did before I took over the sixty — and some grenades. The sun was out and I was pretty much boiling inside my flak jacket and helmet. Not that taking them off was an option. Then I heard that familiar little sound we call the "Laos Pop."

"Time to go, sir," I said.

He was in the middle of calling in an air strike, so he just nodded, holding up one finger for me to wait a minute.

Like we *had* a minute? I was already counting the seconds off in my head, and we didn't have enough time to get to the nearest trench or hole. So I tackled him at the waist — Flaherty blitzes! He sacks the quarterback! The Bengals win! — and slammed him into the ground. Then, dumb guy who follows orders like I am, I made sure that he was completely covered by my body.

It felt like someone hit me across the back with a baseball bat, and then stuck a hot knife in my thigh. I guess the concussion waves were pretty intense, because I blacked out for a minute. I was confused for a few seconds when I opened my eyes, but then I listened to make sure the barrage was over. The Tac Air guy is much smaller than I am, so I hauled him to his feet, and yanked him over to the nearest trench.

He was a little dazed, too, but otherwise fine.

"Thanks, kid," he said. "You okay?"

I thought I was fine, except that my back ached and I could feel some burning on my leg. Doc Jarvis came running over and found a big chunk of shrapnel stuck in the back of my flak jacket and a smaller piece in my thigh. There were some slivers of shrapnel in both of my legs, but they didn't hurt much. I was ready just to slap a bandage on and leave it at that, but Doc didn't like it when he heard I'd passed out.

So — with me swearing the whole time — I ended up on a resupply chopper on my way to Charlie Med.

When we landed, the main base was getting hit hard. Which made me really mad, since I would have been safer back up on the hill. But I knew enough to run for the nearest trench and get down. No wonder they call choppers and cargo planes "Mortar Magnets." I landed on top of some guys who were on their way out of Khe Sanh — either on stretchers, or heading back to the World because their tours were up. We all did some snarling at each other, but then they were tearing across the airstrip to try and jump onto the chopper before it took off. Maybe half of them made it. The others either turned back — or got hit with flying shrapnel. Like Bebop says, this place just isn't healthy.

Getting over to Charlie Med involved another gauntlet of running and diving into trenches, or behind piles of sandbags. The base was really getting *slammed*. They'd been taking heavy fire all day, so Charlie Med was really crowded inside. When they finally got to me, a corpsman read the medical tag Doc Jarvis had filled out and attached to the zipper on my flak jacket. Then he called over a doctor, who did some quick neurological tests to make sure I didn't have a concussion. I already *knew* I didn't, since I've had my bell rung harder than that during football games.

Then, they pulled the shrapnel out of my thigh, and disinfected and bandaged the wound. The doctor moved on to someone else, while the corpsman used tweezers to pick out all of the metal splinters he could find. Can't say I was really thrilled about lying there with my pants around my ankles — but the place was filled with guys a lot worse off than me, so I kept my mouth shut.

Once they'd cleaned me up, I was certified to return to duty — but that doesn't mean I could get a ride back. So, just like that time Bebop and I came down here, I was going to be stuck spending the night.

The back of my flak jacket had been pretty badly shredded, so I helped myself to a better one from the huge pile lying outside Charlie Med and left mine behind. Part of me wondered who had worn it before me, and why he didn't need it anymore — but I decided not to focus on that aspect of it. I was still here, I was mostly in one piece, and I needed a flak jacket to stay that way. Plain and simple.

The base looked completely different from the way it

had a couple of months ago. Most of the above-ground buildings were gone, and there were lots of trenches. There was junk all over the place, too — broken ammo crates, leaking sandbags, empty artillery round cannisters, discarded gear, that kind of stuff. Bunkers were dug much deeper than they had been, and even the smallest ones had overhead cover about six feet deep. Immediately, that made me wonder how come no one ever sent *us* supplies to use for decent bunkers — but, screw it. No matter what anyone else thought, we were doing just fine up on 881S.

Some recoilless rifle guys let me crash on the floor of their bunker for the night. I was so hungry that I didn't even argue when they offered me a can of ham and lima beans.

Okay, I *did* argue — for self-respect — but I kept it short.

Artillery shells and rockets pounded the base just about nonstop, but I've learned to sleep through *anything* — even B-52 air strikes. So, even though some of the rounds seemed to be landing nearby, I wasn't going to sweat it. Either they landed on us, or not. I was too tired to worry about it.

"Man, look at *him*," I heard someone saying, just as I was falling asleep, using part of an ammo crate for a pillow.

"Hill guys are nuts," someone else said.

And proud *of* it.

March 24, 1968

Took me almost all day to get a ride back, and I only managed it because I stayed in the trenches right by the airstrip. I knew — unfortunately — that a medevac would probably be heading out to 881S sooner or later, and I was planning to be on it.

There wasn't much around to scrounge, but I did manage to fill my cargo pockets with a bunch of apples I found. They seemed to be pretty fresh, and it was better than nothing.

When I found my way onto a medevac, the crew chief thought I was insane for going back voluntarily. When a few .51-caliber rounds ripped through the side of the chopper, I thought *he* was insane for doing this every day. Halfway back, I got scared, wondering who had gotten hurt. What if it was Bebop? Or the Professor? Or — we were already hovering over the LZ, and I leaped out, trying to land on my good leg.

The two WIAs were both from Hotel Company. One of the guys was still walking, but he had bandages wrapped around his head and right eye. The other guy had a sucking chest wound, which meant that he was an emergency. If he got to Charlie Med fast enough, though, he would probably be okay. I helped get the stretcher aboard, then ran for the trench. Doc Jarvis — who had been at the other end of the stretcher — jumped in right after me.

"Any concussion?" he asked.

"Nope," I said.

"Did you let them take a look at your bad ear?" he asked.

I was so used to not being able to hear right out of it, that I hadn't even thought to mention it at Charlie Med. "Nope," I said.

Doc Jarvis shook his head. "You're a putz, Mighty Mouse."

"Yep," I said.

When I got back to my position, I found Bebop lying in our bunny hole, playing his mouthpiece and singing "The Khe Sanh Blues." That's a song he made up weeks ago, complete with a little mouthpiece solo in the middle. The big finish goes: *If I gotta choose, I'll take them Khe Sanh Blues.* Although I like the *"It's all over the news, that we've got the Khe Sanh Blues"* part the best.

Pretty catchy tune, actually. I sing it sometimes, too.

He saw me, and a smile spread across his face. "Maria!" he said. "You're back from the Abbey!"

"I'm not supposed to run away from my problems anymore," I said. "I'm supposed to *face* them."

Bebop cracked up. "You're a fool, you know that, Patrick?"

"Yeah," I said, and gave him an apple. "I've heard."

●●●●●●●●●●

March 29, 1968

Typical resupply snafu today. The choppers dropped a couple of pallets on No Man's Land, like usual. We left them there until after dark, because we assumed it was just ammo and C rations, and cans of water.

Come to find out, they'd dropped us a whole load of ice cream in individual Dixie Cups — and it had completely melted. Didn't stop us from eating it, of course. We're all sick as dogs now — it's been too long since we've had normal food like that, so it was way too rich — but it was worth it.

Every bite.

April 1, 1968

Operation Pegasus officially began today. Marine combat engineers are going to work to re-open Route 9, all the way out to the coast, and then the Army — 1st Air Cav, I think — is going to come and "relieve" us. Oh, yeah, we'll be *real* relieved when we see a bunch of doggies show up. But I just want to break out of here, and go out to 881N and get some payback. All those mortars and rockets? All the guys we've lost? We owe it to them to go out and get rid of every last NVA soldier out there.

Rotgut wants to use the M-60, and have me go back to a regular rifle. Says he has more time in-country, and he's trained for it, so I should give it up already. But I've gotten to like having that much firepower, so I just said, nope. He offered to fight me for it, but I said, nope. I figure if I've been doing all the work cleaning and oiling it all these months, I've earned the right to keep it.

Told him he could be my assistant, if he wanted. Somewhere in among all the swearing, I think he said no. Stomped off down the trench, then came stomping back.

"You know, you fire it pretty good," he said. "For a dumb, grungy mick."

"When there is a wrong to right, Mighty Mouse will join the fight," I said, checking the inside of the barrel to make sure that it was absolutely, completely, perfectly clean.

Rotgut just shook his head and stomped off again.

"If we start patrolling again, I'll let you carry the tripod and ammo!" I yelled after him.

He called me about ten more names I'd never want my mother to hear, and then disappeared into his bunny hole.

I think the guy's warming up to me. I really do.

April 3, 1968

Audrey wrote back to me! Two pages, both sides!

Not that I got excited about it, or happy, or read it six times in a row. Nothing like that at all.

She wrote that she was really glad to hear from me, and had been wondering how I was doing. She was actually going to call me when she was home for Christmas break — she's a freshman at Smith College — but then, she heard from someone that I was already over here. She sounds like she's really worried that I'm at Khe Sanh, because she's read so much about it lately, and she told me to be careful at least once on every page. She also wanted to know if I'd mind if she kept writing to me.

Mind?

She really likes college, but hasn't decided what she wants to major in. Literature, she thinks. The other girls are really smart (okay, her exact words were "most of the women here are extremely intelligent"), but she's worried that she doesn't quite fit in, because she doesn't have fifteen cashmere sweaters or a stack of charge cards, and she didn't spend the summer after graduation in Europe, visiting art museums.

No, she spent the summer working at the Pig & Whistle Diner. Before I went to boot camp, I would go by there — well, kind of a lot. I always told her it was because they made such good chicken croquettes.

Which they actually do.

The rest of the letter was filled with news about people we both knew from the neighborhood, and from high school. The only time she mentioned Keith was to say that he was off at the University of Pennsylvania, but she hadn't heard from him recently.

All right!

Finally, at the very end, she wrote that she wished I *had* told her I thought she was cool.

Damn. I wish I had, too. More than ever.

Later --

Tonight was one of our C ration stew nights. When we were only being issued one meal a day and had to conserve every bite, we never bothered doing anything fancy. A little Tabasco sauce, some salt, and that was about it. Most of the time, we didn't even take the time to heat them up — we were just too hungry. But now that supplies aren't as scarce, we're being a little more creative.

The Professor and Pugsley have the biggest bunny hole, so usually, the squad hangs out in that area of the trench. I'm starting to get used to most of the new guys, and we're even finding nicknames for them. Snuffy, this doughy kid out of West Virginia. Rat-Boy, who holds the company record for the number of rats killed in one night — twenty-six. And he even got three of them with a *sling-shot*. Motormouth, a real yappy kid from Watts in Los Angeles, who — big surprise — never seems to stop talking. Twenty-four hours a day. I don't think he sleeps. But he's so friendly that you have to like the kid. Logan, who we might start calling "Grunt," because that's all he ever does — even when you ask him a direct question.

And Bosco, who got his name from a brand of chocolate syrup, because his parents are always sending him bottles of it from home.

We used two different helmets to make our stews. One was a few cans of boned chicken and sliced pork, combined with water, cream substitutes, and about ten cans of cheese spread. When we heated it up, the cheese and cream substitute melted into a lumpy sort of sauce. And Tabasco sauce, of course. We go through *a lot* of Tabasco sauce. Steak sauce, too. If we can get it.

Pugsley worked as a short-order cook back in the World, so on C rat stew nights, we let him take charge. And Pugsley *loves* being in charge. He loves it so much that I'm really glad the Professor is our squad leader, instead of him. Pugsley might get a little too carried away. I like him, but he's really gung-ho.

Our other stew was mostly beef. Beef with spiced sauce, beef and potatoes, meatballs and beans. Throw enough cans in, and you can feed a lot of guys. The potatoes always taste sort of raw, so we call the beef and potatoes C rations "beef and rocks." Motormouth's mother had sent him a jar of pickled onions in his last package, so we added those, too. Pugsley broke off pieces of canned white bread and rolled them into little balls, which he put on top of the beef stew. Claimed that they were now dumplings.

I don't know if any of that sounds good, but it tasted just fine to me. Then again, *all* food tastes fine to me, so what do I know?

One thing you have to like about new guys — lots of them have brand-new radios they bought at the PX, and they stock up on fresh batteries, too. All we have to do is wrap some comm wire around the antennas, string it up to improve the reception, and then we have *tunes*. Bebop keeps saying, grim as hell, that there isn't even one damn jazz fan anywhere in Vietnam. No one ever disagrees with him.

Our two main choices on the radio are AFVN and Hanoi Hannah. Hanoi Hannah is sort of like Tokyo Rose in World War II. The enemy recruits women — there must be more than one, although she always sounds the same — who have these really sexy voices. They come on, and give us all this propaganda about how the "American GIs should throw down their weapons" and that kind of thing. In the gospel according to Hannah, we're evil imperialists who will soon be vanquished by our brave and completely superior enemy. She goes on and on like that. She likes to mention actual unit names and locations — which can be creepy. She's even talked about our hill before, and how little time we have to live before we are crushed by her brothers in arms. Right after that, she played the song "Nowhere to Run, Nowhere to Hide." We thought it was really funny.

But once she stops talking, she plays great music. Lots of rock and roll. *Much* better than AFVN, where they mostly play pop songs, and have commercials about how important it is for us to clean our weapons and wear our helmets. Support the *chieu hoi* program. Protect ourselves from VD. And no matter how bad things are out in the bush, they always report that "American casualties were light." I'd like to see them come up *here*, and say that.

Tonight, Hannah was on a roll, and we were singing along to most of the songs. "Wild Thing." "Woolly Bully." "Dirty Water." That one's all about Boston! "Twentieth Century Fox." Since there's not exactly anything secret about our being here on the hill, the skipper is usually pretty good about letting us crank the volume up before it gets dark, and we have to go out on LPs and start guarding the lines.

Just after the sun went down, she put on my favorite song. *Everyone's* favorite song.

You really haven't lived until you've seen a hundred Marines singing "We've Gotta Get Out of This Place" along with the Animals, and playing air guitar with their M-16s.

On days like today, Vietnam doesn't seem so bad.

April 5, 1968

We never hear anything about what's going on back in the World, except in letters that are days, and usually weeks, old. But today, we found out from AFVN that Dr. Martin Luther King was assassinated in Memphis, Tennessee. The shooter was a white man.

As soon as we heard the news, Bebop went off by himself. I wasn't sure I should go after him, but after a while, I did.

He was lying in our bunny hole with his fists clenched. When he saw me, he scowled.

"Don't even *think* of telling me you're sorry a proud black man got killed," he said.

I had been planning to say something exactly like that, so I just nodded. It would have made things worse if I'd walked away, so I sat down in the trench with my back against one dirt wall and propped my boots up on the other side.

Bebop lit up a cigarette — and didn't offer me one. First time that's ever happened, since we always share everything. He smoked about half of it before he looked over at me.

"Just tell me that you're sorry a *great* man got killed," he said.

"I'm sorry a great man got killed," I said.

And I am.

April 8, 1968

The big news today? The 1st Air Cav officially arrived at the main base and "rescued" us. The besieged, desperate Marines. Yeah. Sure. Like we needed rescuing. All we've needed for weeks now is enough damn supplies — and permission to go *look* for the NVA, instead of waiting for them to try and get the nerve up to come after us. But, how much you want to bet the doggies think they're big, brave heroes for showing up here where they aren't wanted?

There were Hueys filling the skies near the main base today — because doggies don't like to walk. And since the sun went down, we've seen flares go up about every minute.

Looks to me like those Army guys are afraid of the dark. . . .

April 10, 1968

Army doggies are the luckiest guys in the world. There was no incoming down at the main base yesterday — not one round. First time that's happened since January. We got a lot up here, and medevaced three more guys, but the NVA left the Air Cav alone. Ignored them completely. That just figures, doesn't it? Some guys get all the luck.

Starting today, we're running patrols again. *Finally*. The skipper wants us to pace ourselves, since we've been cooped up for so long and everyone's lost a bunch of weight. He must be worried that we're out of shape, but we're ready to go. Let's see if the NVA are willing to take us on face to face. And if they're not, we'll *chase* them.

• • • • • • • • • • •

Later --

Okay, we're out of shape. Lots of panting and gulping water and trying not to get heat exhaustion today.

And that was just me.

I'll never admit it to Rotgut, but humping the M-60 is a real butt-kicker. It's *heavy*. He saw me stagger a little on our way back up to the top of the hill, and he just laughed. I pretended that I'd slipped on a rock.

We didn't have any contact out there today, and, well — maybe that didn't break my heart. Yeah, I want payback, but that doesn't mean I want a bunch of people shooting at me from close range. If they *do*, I'm ready for them, but I figure anyone who really *wants* to be in a fire-fight . . . hasn't been in one before.

The terrain has really changed, because of all the air strikes and fire missions and everything. Those green hills are now full of big bomb craters, and a lot of the jungle growth has been completely burned away. I remember how beautiful it was when we first got here, but now, with all of the ground so torn up, it looks like a moon made of red clay. An ugly moon.

Right down at the base of our hill, we found this huge — and I mean, *huge* — empty complex of trenches, fighting holes, and freshly dug caves. As far as I could tell, the NVA have been digging down there — so close we should probably have been able to *smell* them — for weeks. They must have been planning to over-run 881S for real.

When we first saw it — and then realized how big and well-prepared the position was — everyone got really quiet for a minute. After all, we *saw* what it was like those nights when 861 and 861A got attacked. But then we all snapped out of it, started searching each and every hole and tunnel we could find, and got ready to destroy as much of it as we could with C-4 and grenades. Fire missions, and maybe air strikes, will take care of the rest. Some guys were even running around looking for souvenirs. I found this dented little metal rice bowl and a belt buckle with a star on it. Even though I didn't really want the stuff, I stuck them in one of my cargo pockets, since everyone else was.

I'd be lying if I didn't say that the entire time we were there, my stomach hurt.

A lot.

April 13, 1968

The hill is getting really crowded. During the past few days, the whole battalion has been moved over here to 881S, and there isn't enough room. So, we're just expanding the perimeter and spreading further out onto the nearby ridges.

The NVA must have been excited to see so many nice, new targets, because we've been taking a lot of incoming rounds and machine gun fire. And yeah, quite a few casualties, too. I guess I'm used to it by now — but you *never* get used to it.

First thing tomorrow, the whole battalion is moving out to assault 881N. We know they're out there, since they keep shooting at us. We were really pumped up — until we found out that our company had been assigned the reserve position.

In other words, we're second-string. Back-ups. On the bench.

Even the skipper doesn't get to go. His promotion just came down, so they brought in a new company commander. The skipper's still up here on the hill, though, which makes me feel better. The new commander is probably okay — but he's *new*.

It's going to be hard to watch everyone *but* us head out there tomorrow.

April 14, 1968

They took the hill. While we watched. It was frustrating, but we still let out a hell of a cheer when the word came back that a kid from Kilo Company had climbed a tree and raised an American flag up on top of 881N. Throughout the fight, our hill laid down a constant stream of 60 mm and 81mm mortars, howitzer rounds, and recoilless rifle fire. The guys on the .50 caliber machine guns got a good work-out, too.

The rest of us? Well, we mostly just watched. Except when the NVA managed to fire off a few rockets and some machine gun fire at us, and we had to take cover. One of the recoilless rifle gun teams got hit, and we had to call a chopper in to send four badly wounded guys out. As usual, the guns and mortars were firing so much that they overheated, and we did our usual "cool them down" techniques. It doesn't even seem gross anymore — we just do it automatically.

In the meantime, the other companies swarmed all over 881N, and wasted every NVA they could find. I don't think that there were as many as they expected, but the ones who *were* there fought hard. The rest of the NVA retreated, I guess. In the afternoon, our platoon was allowed to be a rear escort for the battalion command group, but by then, all of the fighting was pretty much over.

I heard six of our guys got killed out there, and there were maybe twenty WIAs who had to be evacuated. Casualties for the NVA were about ten or twenty times higher than that — which they just love to hear back at Division.

Doesn't change the fact that six families back in the World are about to find out that their sons died on Easter.

Yeah, today was Easter Sunday. It didn't feel right for there to be a big battle on such an important day. But, it also didn't feel right when we went patrolling two days ago on Good Friday. Felt even *worse* when I had to fire my M-60 at a couple of tree-lines, after we kept getting sniper fire.

Last year on Good Friday, I got excused from baseball practice, because it wouldn't have been right to play. My mother has always been really strict about us showing respect on religious holidays, *especially* Good Friday. And this year? Well, we didn't find any bodies or anything, but for all I know, I might have killed someone out there. Maybe even more than one person. On Good Friday.

If you really thought about it, this war could make you completely crazy.

April 17, 1968, Khe Sanh Combat Base

We've turned 881S over to another company, and now we're down on the main base, waiting to head back to the rear for a few days. I'm not sure where we're going after that, but it'll probably be somewhere near the DMZ. The Rockpile, maybe, or Con Thien. Bebop's betting on Leatherneck Square, while the Professor is guessing that we'll just end up humping through rice paddies and villages somewhere near the coast. It's a whole different war over there, so it'll be a big change.

The base is pretty deserted, since operations are winding down. But the NVA big guns over in Laos are still firing artillery rounds. I can't wait to get out of here. I'm *sick* of Khe Sanh.

April 18, 1968
Quang Tri, Republic of South Vietnam

Like the man said, we're finally in the rear, with the gear. *Outstanding.* Our whole company was lifted out of Khe Sanh this afternoon, and they flew us to Quang Tri. Quang Tri is this huge — and *really safe* — base, so it's great to be here.

When the choppers showed up to get us, we had to dodge through another mortar and artillery barrage. The NVA were just saying good-bye, I guess. And as we took off, we could hear a few antiaircraft rounds slapping against the side of the chopper. Talk about feeling helpless. You just have to sit there, and hope they miss. This time, luckily, they did.

Then we landed at Quang Tri, and almost no one there was wearing flak jackets or helmets. A lot of Marines weren't even carrying their *rifles*. It felt almost like being at some stateside base. On top of that, the Marine Corps Band was right by the edge of the airstrip, waiting for us. When we walked down the ramp of CH-53 chopper, the band started playing "The Marines' Hymn." It was pretty cool — I swear I actually felt chills when I heard the song.

There we are, completely filthy, our uniforms all torn and rotted, and so thin that what was left of our clothes was hanging off us. Most of the guys have beards now, because there was never enough water for people to shave — but even though I *really tried*, I couldn't manage to grow one. I still figure I looked pretty damn grungy. Anyway, the band was playing, and we were all standing at attention and saluting.

I'm really lucky to be so cool, or else the whole thing might have made me feel a little choked up.

When the band finished, we were supposed to head onto the base to get showers and everything — but then, I looked at Bebop. You've never seen such a *hungry* expression in your whole life. He broke out of the ranks and practically ran over to one of the sax players. The Professor and I weren't sure what he was going to do, so we followed him, in case he needed back-up.

"Hey, man, can I try your horn for a minute?" he asked.

The sax player — all neat and clean, in a perfect uniform — looked kind of scared, and moved away a couple of steps. "Sorry," he said. "No can do."

"Come on, *please?*" Bebop said. "I can't *tell* you how much it would mean to me, Marine."

The guy just kept shaking his head and moving away. He was looking around, like he thought someone might come and rescue him.

"Come on, troops!" our new CO was barking. "Leave 'im alone, and let's move out!"

Bebop yanked his mouthpiece out of his pocket. "Just for a minute? Please?"

The Professor took out an NVA canteen he'd picked up on patrol, and when I saw that, I dug out the rice bowl and belt buckle I'd found the other day.

"Let him play, kid," I said. "We'll swap you these for five minutes on the horn."

The kid looked tempted when he saw *actual battlefield* NVA souvenirs. Stuff like that is worth a lot in the rear. "I really can't," he said. "We're not —" Then, he noticed Bebop's mouthpiece. "Hey, is that an *Otto Link?*"

Bebop nodded, sticking an old reed in his mouth to get it damp enough to play.

"You a player, man?" the kid asked.

Bebop nodded, sucking away on the reed. "That your good horn?"

The kid looked down at his sax. "Are you kidding? Bring my good horn in-country? I got a Balanced Action at home."

They started talking about saxophone brands and something called set-ups and stuff like that, while the kid fished out a fresh reed and gave it to Bebop.

"Here," he said. "Try this one."

Bebop looked it over, then nodded. "That'll do," he said, and stuck it in his mouth for a minute.

By the time he had borrowed the kid's neck-strap and was holding the saxophone, most of the company had gathered around to see what was going to happen. Bebop ran his fingers down the keys, and smiled. Then, he took a deep breath and started to play. And it was amazing. He started off with this real swingy version of "The Marines' Hymn," and even the band came over to listen.

Then, he just — took off. I don't really know how to describe it, but the sound kind of soared. I thought I could hear the song "My Favorite Things" somewhere in there, but he was going off in all different directions, and I suddenly knew what he meant when he'd told me about riffs and licks and improvising all those days and nights on 881S.

"Is that bebopping?" I asked the Professor softly.

The kid saxophone player heard me. "Man, is it *ever*," he said, his voice awed.

I don't know how long he played, but the whole world just seemed to slow down and listen. Everyone nearby on the base, anyway. All I could think was that I felt really lucky to know him. He'd talked so much about music, that I'd figured he had to be pretty good, but I had *no idea*. This was — this was just plain *magic*.

When he stopped, I blinked, and it took a few seconds to remember that I was in Vietnam, standing next to an airbase, in the middle of what had become a really big crowd. Everyone was clapping and yelling stuff at him, but Bebop was so cool that he just put his mouthpiece in his pocket, took off the neck strap, and handed the sax back to the kid.

"Nice horn," he said, and walked away.

Man, you don't *get* any cooler than that.

Later --

After that, we were herded off for showers — actual showers! — and fresh uniforms. When I tried to take off my T-shirt, it shredded right in my hands, leaving just the collar hanging around my neck. And my pants weren't much better. When we dropped what was left of our old uniforms on the ground, *flies* gathered. Seriously. And the smell must have been intense, because people walking by winced and covered their noses.

First, they made us line up and some guys wearing gas masks sprayed this insecticide all over us. Didn't make much sense to me, but the Professor said it was to get rid of lice. Oh, yeah, *there's* a nice thought. After that, we lined up for showers. I wish there had been more water, because I would have stayed under those showers all afternoon. Layer after layer of clay and filth came off, but when I got out, my skin still looked reddish and felt gritty.

I guess it'll take a lot more than one shower to get rid of Khe Sanh.

It was almost hard to recognize people without their beards and no longer covered by dirt. We were all laughing and fooling around and feeling absolutely great in clean uniforms. So what if most of them didn't fit right?

Battalion had set it up so that a bunch of cooks were fixing steaks for us on these grills made out of fifty-five gallon metal drums. Boy, they smelled great. There was Black Label beer, too, which was what we all grabbed first. And someone had hooked up speakers, so we had rock and roll blaring out over the compound.

It was really fun. We were all hanging out, and eating and drinking, and trying to forget the last few months. It's hard to believe, but only nineteen of the Golf Company guys who originally went up on 881S made it. *Nineteen.* That's out of a couple of hundred guys. Everyone else was either killed or wounded. And even among the nineteen of us left, most of us got injured at least once. Wow. I knew things were bad up there, but I'd never actually heard the numbers before. Lots of our replacements got killed and wounded, too, so who knows how high the casualties *really* were.

After we ate, they told us to drop our gear off in this row of tents set aside for Golf Company. That's where we'd be sleeping tonight, and maybe even for the next week or so. No one was quite sure where the battalion was going to be sent, or what we would be doing when we got there. No one much cared, either.

The idea of being in a regular hardback tent, on a cot, above the ground, seemed totally foreign. The first thing we all did was haul out our entrenching tools, so that we could dig in. We might not be in the field, but that was no reason to get lazy — or careless. But we had barely gotten started, when some officer yelled at us to cut it out. I guess he didn't want us messing up his nice, neat rows of tents or something. We just ignored him, but he was really bent out of shape, so finally the skipper told us to stop. The rules are different back in the rear, mainly because there *are* rules back in the rear.

It seemed stupid to us, but we were really tired, so we didn't argue. Much. We ended up lying down on our bunks, sipping beer or Cokes, and talking. Without even discussing it, we all knew that we didn't want to talk about the hill tonight — or Vietnam, or anything else that might spoil the mood. So we talked about girls, and more girls, and the best meals we'd ever had, and what cool cars we were all going to buy when we got back to the World, and stuff like that. Mostly, of course, we talked about girls.

We're supposed to be issued new flak jackets tomorrow, because our old ones are so worn-out that they're practically useless. My helmet's still okay, although the BFD is really faded, and Mighty Mouse has a tear right through his cape. Maybe they'll give me a new camo cover or something. I could use a pair of boots, too — mine have holes, the leather is all scarred, and the canvas is stained practically white from perspiration instead of green.

By about 2300, almost everyone was asleep. Pugsley had been snoring away since about 2100, which we all thought was pretty funny. In the field, you try not to snore, because it might give away your position. So, I guess he's making up for lost time. Since we could pick any bunk we wanted, our tent was mostly filled with old guys, with only a few of the newer ones. I don't know; I guess we just felt like hanging together tonight. Celebrating the fact that we'd made it down from 881S alive.

The Professor talked a little, but mostly, he had been lying on his rack reading. Batteries had been scarce for so long, but we didn't have to worry about that here. The base has *electricity*. Rotgut seemed just the same as always — yep, you got it — *mean*, and he drank about as much as the rest of us put together. So I'm not sure if he was asleep, or if he'd just passed out.

Bebop and I were almost out of cigarettes, so we took turns smoking the last couple, passing them back and forth to each other after each drag.

"You were something today," I said. "I almost wasn't embarrassed to know you."

Bebop grinned, since he knew perfectly well that that meant I'd been really proud of him.

"So — was that jazz?" I asked. "It sort of sounded like 'My Favorite Things.'"

He laughed, exhaled some smoke, and handed the cigarette to me. "Do me a favor, man. Promise me you'll sit down for a couple hours someday and listen to Mr. John Coltrane."

Fair enough. "Will do," I said.

We talked until he fell asleep, too. So I decided to take a few minutes, and write about everything that happened today. It was really peaceful in the tent, and except for snoring, the only sound was the Professor turning pages in his book.

I guess I *am* a little nervous about where we're going next. What if it's even *worse* than Khe Sanh? Hard to imagine that it could be, but if I've learned anything over here, it's that this is a *really* bad war. I know all wars are bad, but this one seems — I don't know. I wish I could sit down and talk to my father, and my uncles, and find out what *their* wars were really like. This time, I know they'd tell me the truth. The whole story — even the horrible parts. But I bet they'd also tell me about their buddies, and how close they all were, and how after a while, you'd do *anything* for them.

With all of the bad parts of war — this war — every war? — at least you're together with a bunch of great, brave guys who you trust more than —

April 21, 1968
18th Surgical Hospital,
Quang Tri, Republic of South Vietnam

When I woke up, I couldn't figure out where I was. Everything smelled funny, I was thirsty as hell, and some guy was leaning over me. No idea who he was — just a guy. Complete stranger, really blurry.

"Hey, man," he said. Looked surprised. "You're back!"

Back? Back where?

"Don't worry, troop, it's okay," he said. "You're going home."

Going home? What?

Can't write anymore now. I can't *think*. I don't *want* to think.

• • • • • • • • • •

Later --

I'm going home — and I don't care. Apparently, I'm all messed up — and I don't care. The last thing I remember is lying on my rack in the tent, writing. I was having trouble keeping my eyes open, so I was about to put my pen down.

Then, I heard it. The shriek, and the whistle. The sound of a *rocket*. Everyone woke up instantly, because we knew that sound — and we knew that it was heading straight for us. It must have hit us then, because I don't remember any of us getting out of the tent in time. The beams came crashing down, guys were screaming, and — that's all I remember.

I woke up here in the hospital. They had me all hooked up to tubes and needles, and I guess I was pretty critical, because the doctors and everyone seemed sort of shocked that I was conscious. I had a tube in my throat, but I got so upset that they took it out.

The first thing I asked was where the other guys were, and if they were all right, but they either didn't know — or didn't want to tell me — because no one would answer me. I guess I took a lot of shrapnel in the chest, because of all the tubes and bandages. In fact, my whole left side looks — and feels — like it got chewed up. They keep putting on fresh bandages, but the red comes staining through in a couple of minutes. One of the corpsman told me that my lung was punctured. Sucking chest wound.

Every few hours, someone comes and shoots me full of morphine. I know I'm in pain, but they have me on so many drugs that I can't really focus on it. They tried to take this book away from me, but I started yelling and swearing, so they left me alone. I had trouble even finding it at first, and thought it might be lost, but it turned out to be in this little canvas bag hanging next to my bed. It was in my shirt pocket when I got hit, and one of the doctors says that might have saved my life, because there's shrapnel stuck in the cover which probably would have gone right into my heart. The same doctor also says that my left leg is in really bad shape, but there's a pretty good chance they might not have to amputate it.

A pretty good chance.

I'm surrounded by guys who are all in critical condition, so I guess this is intensive care. The guy in the bed across from me is in a world of hurt — his head and eyes all covered with bandages, and both legs gone just above the knees. He seems to respond when they talk to him, so I guess he doesn't have brain damage, but I heard someone saying that he's going to be completely blind.

Oh, God, it hurts. It hurts a lot. Where's that son-of-a-bitch with the morphine? I can't even — I just wish someone would tell me where my buddies are.

I have to stop writing — this is too hard.

• • • • • • • • • •

April 22, 1968

Rotgut came to see me first thing this morning. He had a bandage wrapped around his hand, but other than that, he was fine. When he saw me, his eyes got all bright and he kept swallowing.

"I'm glad you're here, man," I said. "Where is everyone? Are they okay?"

He actually started crying and couldn't talk for a minute.

So I knew it was bad. I forgot how much everything hurt, because I knew he was going to tell me stuff I didn't want to hear.

"Did anyone else get hurt?" I asked.

He stared at me, and then pointed across the aisle at the blind guy with the missing legs.

Oh, God. "Who is it?" I asked.

"The Professor," he said.

I was ten feet away from the Professor — my buddy — and with all of those bandages covering his face and head, *I hadn't even recognized him.* Oh, God. I didn't ask if he was going to be okay, because I could *see* that he wasn't.

So I waited to hear the rest.

Our tent took a direct hit from the rocket. A few guys were able to walk away with minor injuries, but the Professor and I were seriously wounded. In fact, neither of us had been expected to survive that first night.

And then, still crying, Rotgut told me the hard part. Six

Marines were killed, including Pugsley, Motormouth —
and Bebop.

Bebop.

"God, I am really sorry, man," Rotgut said. "I'm
really —" He was having trouble talking, so he just stared
down at the floor. "I'm sorry, man, I gotta go," he said in a
really low voice, and walked away, still crying.

Bebop.

Oh, God, *not* Bebop.

Later --

The Professor was transferred to the U.S.S. *Repose*, the
hospital ship anchored out in the South China Sea. I guess
they have some big eye specialist out there. I was able to
say good-bye to him, and they even wheeled him close
enough so that I could shake his hand. I was scared that he
might not know who I was, but he gripped my hand and
whispered, "Don't worry, Mighty Mouse. It'll be okay."

Yeah. Sure it will.

They were preparing me to be evacuated out on the
next flight to the general hospital in Japan, when the
skipper showed up. He looked ten years older than he
had the last time I saw him, and I thought for a minute
that he might cry, too — especially when he found out
that he had just missed the Professor. Apparently, he had

come to see us a couple of times before, but we had both been unconscious.

"How you doing, son?" he asked.

"Fine, sir," I answered. "Thank you, sir." Once a Marine, always a Marine.

I guess he could tell that I couldn't really bring myself to talk, because he just sat down next to me, while they were getting me ready to go. Told me how proud he was of me — and all the guys — and what an honor it had been to serve as our commander, and how very sorry he was. I nodded in all the right places, and tried to smile at him.

The corpsmen were transferring me to a gurney now, and the skipper stood up.

"Take care of yourself," he said, and paused. "You're one fine Marine, Patrick."

Then they took me away.

On the plane --

Bebop. Why Bebop? Why *anyone*, but why Bebop? Why not *me*, instead? I *wish* it had been me.

I'm going home.

The best friend I've ever had isn't.

What else is there to say?

● ● ● ● ● ● ● ● ● ● ●

Epilogue

●●●●●●●●●●●

Officially, the battle of Khe Sanh lasted for seventy-seven long days. More than 100,000 tons of bombs were dropped in the area during this time frame, and at least 150,000 artillery rounds were fired at the enemy. At the time, it was the most intense aerial bombardment in the history of warfare. But within weeks, the main base at Khe Sanh had been completely torn down, and was abandoned by United States forces. The territory the Marines had defended so fiercely, spilling their own blood in the process, was ultimately given up without a fight.

Patrick Flaherty was evacuated from the 18th Surgical Hospital in South Vietnam to a military hospital at Camp Zama, in Japan. Once his condition had stabilized, he was transferred back to the United States, where he spent eight months recuperating at the Philadelphia Naval Hospital. Although his leg was almost amputated on three separate occasions, the doctors managed to save it. And after months of therapy, Patrick was able to get his strength back and learn how to walk again.

His family drove down to Philadelphia to visit him as

often as possible, and during her summer break, his friend Audrey Taylor began coming, too. When he was finally released, Patrick returned to Boston. After a few more months of recuperating at home, he enrolled in Boston College for the fall semester in 1969. He was strong enough to play football again — but the game no longer seemed very interesting, or important.

Antiwar protests were everywhere, and even with long hair and a mustache, as an ex-Marine, Patrick did not feel comfortable being on a college campus. So, he dropped out near the end of his freshman year. His family was very supportive, but Patrick spent a lot of time by himself, not sure if he had enough energy to figure out what he was going to do with the rest of his life. Sometimes, he wasn't even sure if he cared enough to try. But by now, he was dating Audrey seriously, and with her encouragement, his confidence began to come back.

He took the city exam for the Boston Fire Department, and spent months working out so that he would be able to pass the physical examinations and go through the training program. He was hired as a member of the department, passed the academy with flying colors, and was assigned to a ladder company at a busy firehouse in Roxbury. He also asked Audrey to marry him, and she accepted.

Patrick stayed in the Boston Fire Department for more than twenty-five years, rising to the rank of District Chief. He and Audrey had four children, and Patrick was pleased, and a little surprised, when his son — and one of his three daughters — followed him into the Fire Department. They became the fifth generation of Flahertys to serve as members of the BFD. Privately, Patrick has always hoped that, one day, at least one of his grandchildren will continue the tradition.

After he retired from the fire department, and Audrey left her job teaching English at Dorchester High School, they moved to a small town in northern New Hampshire, where they still live today. Patrick is the chief of the local volunteer fire department, and he spends most of his free time hiking and skiing. He rarely discusses his time in Vietnam, but he's not sorry that he went, and he's proud to have been a United States Marine.

There is one promise he made in Vietnam which he has always kept — and always will. Ever since he was released from the Philadelphia Naval Hospital, back in 1969, Patrick has made a point of sitting down and listening to some jazz — John Coltrane or one of the other great saxophone players — every single day, without fail.

And every single time, it makes him sad.

Life in America
in 1968

Historical Note

● ● ● ● ● ● ● ● ● ● ●

The Vietnam War began much earlier than most people realize, and for many Americans, it can be argued that even today, it has never ended. There are different opinions about how and why the United States became involved in the war, and even more opinions about whether this was right or wrong, and how our country's history was changed as a result. The country was — and is — sharply divided about the war. The bitter and angry feelings which intensified throughout the 1960s continue to simmer decades later, as America tries to come to terms with a war that became a nightmare.

Vietnam has had a long history of fighting for its independence from much larger and more powerful nations. For centuries, the little country struggled against its powerful neighbor to the north, China. Then, by the late 1800s, Vietnam had — against its will — become a colony of France. The entire Vietnam-Laos-Cambodia area was called French Indochina.

During World War II, Japan moved in to occupy Vietnam for geographical and strategic reasons. This concerned the United States a great deal, and for the first time, America began providing financial aid to Indochina (Vietnam).

When World War II came to an end, Vietnam was still considered a French colony, and a determined Vietnamese leader named Ho Chi Minh vowed that Vietnam was going to achieve its independence once and for all. He appealed to then-United States President, Harry S Truman, for help. Although America did not want to support French colonial rule, encouraging Ho Chi Minh and his Communist beliefs also seemed like a poor policy decision. So, the United States did not respond to Ho Chi Minh's overtures.

With the help of a young general named Giap, Ho Chi Minh authorized a guerilla military force called the Viet Minh to form. Soon, the French Indochina War had begun. Ho Chi Minh and the Viet Minh were located in the northern part of Vietnam, and they started attacking the less militant, southern half of Vietnam, where many French installations were located.

By now, Dwight D. Eisenhower was the President of the United States. He had very strong negative beliefs about Communism, and felt that America should battle against this political evil in all corners of the world. President Eisenhower and his administration were concerned that the Soviet Union and China were potentially serious threats to American security, and that all forms of Communism should be eliminated. The United States had become involved in what was called the Cold War with the Soviet Union during the early 1950s, and our troops were also fighting in the Korean War during this same time period. Now it seemed as though America would intervene in Vietnam, as well.

Deciding that French colonialism was the lesser of two evils, the United States began sending significant aid, as well as military advisors, to Vietnam. The military advisors were assigned the task of helping develop and train a Southern Vietnamese army. But despite America's efforts, the Viet Minh were clearly winning the war.

In 1954, General Giap's troops won a decisive and dramatic battle against France at an isolated outpost called Dien Bien Phu. Later that year, a fragile peace was established at a conference in Switzerland known as the Geneva Accords. Vietnam — no longer known as Indochina — was officially divided into two parts. This division was made at the 17th Parallel. (Years later, this would be called the Demilitarized Zone, or DMZ.) Communist North Vietnam was located above the line, and the more democratic South Vietnam was below the dividing line. On paper, South Vietnam was permitted to seek its own form of government and hold free elections. But Ho Chi Minh and his followers were eager to "reform" their fellow countrymen and women.

The Viet Minh were now called the Vietnamese Communists. This term was shortened to the more familiar phrase Viet Cong, or VC. Communist troops began to infiltrate the South, and guerilla attacks and terrorist acts became common. The United States increased the number of American military advisors, and also sent financial aid to the struggling South Vietnamese citizens. Unfortunately, the South Vietnamese soldiers were not developing into an army capable of defending themselves against North Vietnam.

It seemed inevitable that Vietnam would soon be a completely Communist country. Either the United States could step back and allow this to happen — or American troops could be sent in. In 1964, President Lyndon B. Johnson and his advisors had decided that it was time for America to take charge.

In August of 1964, there was a confrontation in the Gulf of Tonkin between North Vietnamese patrol boats and a United States Navy ship. At the time, it was interpreted as an attack against American forces, but it may only have been a minor threat. In any case, the United States Senate and House of Representatives signed a Joint Resolution of Congress protesting this event. This Tonkin Gulf Resolution gave President Johnson permission "to take all necessary measures to repel any . . . attacks against . . . the United States . . . including the use of armed force." President Johnson had vowed not to enlarge the scope of the war, but he ended up ordering bombing missions over North Vietnam and sending large numbers of American troops to South Vietnam. The Vietnam War had begun.

Within a year, there were at least 125,000 American

troops in Vietnam, and the numbers just kept growing. North Vietnam, in addition to its Viet Cong guerilla troops, had created a large North Vietnamese Army to confront their new enemy: the United States. President Johnson's administration and the American military command were planning only to assist their allies, the Army of the Republic of South Vietnam, or ARVN. The United States was planning to help South Vietnam defend itself, without escalating the war by invading North Vietnam, or neighboring Cambodia and Laos.

This strategy made it very easy for the NVA and VC to mount swift "hit-and-run" attacks, and then retreat to safety in areas where American troops could not follow them. These guerilla tactics were difficult to handle. Well aware of typical American strategy, Ho Chi Minh and General Giap decided simply to keep sending in endless numbers of troops, and continue the fight no matter how many casualties they sustained. Therefore, the Vietnam War became known as a war of attrition, or a "body count" war.

The American military, led by General William Westmoreland, assumed that if enough enemy forces were killed, North Vietnam would surrender. At the same time, North Vietnam reasoned that United States citizens would not be able to tolerate watching American soldiers return home in body bags for very long.

The Vietnam War was different for America in another crucial way. During prior wars, communications technology had been much less sophisticated. Reports from the battle-front would show up days later in the newspaper, or in newsreels at movie theaters. But since then, a little invention called television had taken the country by storm. For the first time, Americans could watch a war right from their own living rooms. And they did not like what they saw. It started to be said that America was winning all of their battles in Vietnam, but losing the war where it counted — at home. Antiwar protests became much more common, and Americans on both sides of the issue were increasingly hostile towards one another.

The year 1968 was the turning point. There were about half a million American soldiers in Vietnam, and the war seemed to be getting worse with each passing day. In January of that year, 6,000 Marines at a lonely, little base called Khe Sanh were surrounded by as many as 40,000 North Vietnamese troops. (The actual numbers are unknown.) From President Johnson all the way down to the ordinary citizen, America was riveted by what was being called the worst siege since the terrible French defeat at Dien Bien Phu in 1954.

Then, in late January, during the Tet holiday truce, NVA and VC troops simultaneously attacked cities, villages, and American military bases all over the country. These attacks were so savage and unexpected that the American Embassy was occupied by the enemy for a period of hours. Despite the fact that American soldiers were able to repulse every single one of these attacks (the battle for the city of Hue lasted almost a month), the United States was stunned by this turn of events. The antiwar movement intensified. Increasingly, veterans returning home from Vietnam were treated with great disrespect, and sometimes even cruelty, by Americans who were against the war. Veterans were shocked to find themselves accused of being "baby killers" or "warmongers." Anyone in uniform was treated as an enemy by the antiwar movement.

In late March, President Johnson went on television to announce a bombing halt in North Vietnam, to call for peace, and to say that he would not be running for reelection. That fall, Richard Nixon won the Presidency, campaigning on a platform of "peace with honor." Fierce fighting continued for several more years, but gradually, American troops were withdrawn from Vietnam. This strategy is called "Vietnamization."

By 1973, South Vietnam and its army had essentially been left to fend for itself. In April 1975, Saigon, the capital city of South Vietnam, fell, and the war was finally over.

But the memories in America did not fade, and there were still many bitter feelings among veterans and civilians alike. Stereotypes of crazed, violent Vietnam veterans were all too common on television and in the movies. Many veterans had learned never to discuss their service during the war, and to pretend that none of it had ever happened.

During the 1980s, the Vietnam War began to be reevaluated.

In 1982, the Vietnam War Memorial was dedicated in Washington, DC. As the years passed, Vietnam veterans were seen in a much more positive light, although many people still condemned the war itself. Even today, though, Americans struggle to understand the Vietnam experience and its implications for the future.

One of the most well-known statements about the Vietnam War came from an American officer who said "we had to destroy the village, in order to save it." The world is undeniably a complicated place, with conflicts arising in many countries, for many different reasons. With any luck, in the future, the United States will be able to figure out a way simply to help save all of the villages, including our own, without destroying them.

Military Code of Conduct

● ● ● ● ● ● ● ● ● ● ●

ARTICLE I: I am an American, fighting in the forces which guard my country and our way of life. I am prepared to give my life in their defense.

ARTICLE II: I will never surrender of my own free will. If in command, I will never surrender the members of my command while they still have the means to resist.

ARTICLE III: If I am captured I will continue to resist by all means available. I will make every effort to escape and to aid others to escape. I will accept neither parole nor special favors from the enemy.

ARTICLE IV: If I become a prisoner of war, I will keep faith with my fellow prisoners. I will give no information nor take part in any action which might be harmful to my comrades. If I am senior, I will take command. If not, I will obey lawful orders of those appointed over me and will back them in every way.

ARTICLE V: When questioned, should I become a prisoner of war, I am required to give name, rank, service number, and date of birth. I will evade answering further questions to the utmost of my ability. I will make no oral or written statements disloyal to my country or its allies or harmful to their cause.

ARTICLE VI: I will never forget that I am an American, fighting for freedom, responsible for my actions, and dedicated to the principles which made my country free. I will trust in my God and in the UNITED STATES OF AMERICA.

The Marines' Hymn

From the halls of Montezuma, to the shores of
        Tripoli,
We fight our country's battles in the air, on land
        and sea.
First to fight for right and freedom, and to keep
        our honor clean;
We are proud to claim the title of United States
        Marine.

Our flag's unfurled to every breeze from dawn
        to setting sun.
We have fought in every clime and place, where
        we could take a gun.
In the snow of far off northern lands and in
        sunny tropic scenes,
You will find us always on the job, the United
        States Marines.

Here's health to you and to our Corps which
        we are proud to serve.
In many a strife we've fought for life and never
        lost our nerve.
If the Army and the Navy ever look on
        heaven's scenes,
They will find the streets are guarded by
        United States Marines.

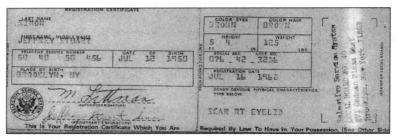

The American government's conscription system during the Vietnam War included draft cards that notified young men that they were being called to service.

U.S. Marines, dropped off by a helicopter, arrive in the hills of Khe Sanh in October 1968.

American servicemen eat their C rations.

Sgt. Joseph Michael Jones of Chattahoochee, Florida, reads his mail while stationed on Hill 881 South in Khe Sanh. The Florida state flag flies behind him.

U.S. Marines wait in a bunker atop a hill at Khe Sanh and watch for enemy activity.

American soldiers lug machine guns up a hill near the Khe Sanh base.

A platoon of U.S. cavalry soldiers patrol the jungles near the Khe Sanh Marine combat base.

On Hill 881, two Marines escort a wounded comrade to a helicopter evacuation pad.

A helicopter delivers a howitzer gun to the U.S. 3rd Marine Division, occupying a hill near the Laos–South Vietnamese border.

A soldier directs a helicopter dropping a sling filled with cases of ice cream on an American hilltop outpost in South Vietnam.

After her village is seized by the Viet Cong, a young Montagnard mother clutches her son as she waits to be evacuated to a nearby hospital.

With his baby strapped to his back, a Montagnard tribesman participates in the joint American–South Vietnamese effort to push back the North Vietnamese Army and the Viet Cong.

185

An American soldier plays on a swingset with a young Vietnamese boy in a playground at the American base in Cu Chi, South Vietnam. It was built by American servicemen as part of a community improvement project.

With his guitar and his M-16 rifle strapped to his back, a Marine awaits his flight out of Khe Sanh.

Almost twenty years after the end of the Vietnam War, a Vietnamese man tends his field in the Khe Sanh Valley. With the fall of Communism in 1991, many Western nations reestablished diplomatic and economic relations with Vietnam. The last country to do so was the United States, in 1995. Vietnam is still a rural and very poor country, though it is rich in culture and natural beauty.

Acknowledgments

● ● ● ● ● ● ● ● ● ● ●

Grateful acknowledgment is made for permission to reprint the following:

Cover Portrait: John E. Wilson, Larry Burrows/Timepix. John Wilson, a U.S. Marine who served in Vietnam in 1966, returned to the United States after the war. He now lives with his wife and sons near Spokane, Washington. This photograph, taken by Larry Burrows, was published in *LIFE* magazine in one of several powerful photo-essays that influenced American sentiment about the war in Vietnam. Burrows was killed in Vietnam while on assignment, and his photographs are still regarded as some of the most moving images of the Vietnam era.

Cover Background: Topham/The Image Works.

Page 180 (top): Draft card, AP/Wide World Photos.
Page 180 (bottom): Helicopter exit, AP/Wide World Photos.
Page 181 (top): C rations, CORBIS.
Page 181 (bottom): Soldier reading mail, Bettmann/CORBIS.
Page 182 (top): Waiting in the bunker, Bettmann/CORBIS.
Page 182 (bottom): Carrying machine guns, AP/Wide World Photos.
Page 183 (top): Jungle patrol, AP/Wide World Photos.
Page 183 (bottom): Carrying wounded Marine, Bettmann/CORBIS.
Page 184 (top): Helicopter dropping guns, Bettmann/CORBIS.
Page 184 (bottom): Ice cream drop, AP/Wide World Photos.
Page 185 (top): Montagnard woman, Bettmann/CORBIS.
Page 185 (bottom): Montagnard tribesman, Bettmann/CORBIS.
Page 186 (top): Soldier on the swing, Bettmann/CORBIS.
Page 186 (bottom): Marine with guitar and gun, Bettmann/CORBIS.
Page 187: Vietnamese farmer, Steve Raymer/CORBIS.

In honor of all of the men and women who served in Vietnam.
• • • • • • • • • •

While the events described and some of the characters in this book may
be based on actual historical events and real people, Patrick Seamus Flaherty
is a fictional character, created by the author, and his journal and its
epilogue are works of fiction.

• • • • • • • • • •

The display type was set in Love Letter Typewriter.
The text type was set in Berling Roman.
Book design by Elizabeth B. Parisi.
Photo research by Dwayne Howard and Zoe Moffitt.

4 5 6 7 8 9 10   23   12 11 10 09 08 07

• • • • • • • • • •